THE CONQUEST OF
THE RED MAN

Corinne Maier

Traduction : Nazanine Nayeri

THE CONQUEST OF THE RED MAN
Corinne Maier

ISBN 978-1903110690

First published in this edition 2021 by Wrecking Ball Press

Copyright © Corinne Maier

Design: humandesign.co.uk

LOTTERY FUNDED | Supported using public funding by
ARTS COUNCIL ENGLAND

Contents

Brussels, January 2016: the starter

It's the first time I'm doing the cleaning. I tidy up, pack, clean, swallow dust. That's it; the boxes are pretty much done. They're stacked in the huge living room, with its elegant stained-glass window that looks out on the street and depicts a bird twirling on a bare tree branch. Moving out: a real nightmare for those who hate using their hands. To hit the ground running, I've studied the *Cleaning for Beginners* handbook. "Always use cloths, brushes and mops from the cleanest to the dirtiest, from highest to lowest, from right to left." Useful advice to learn the ways of the world properly, in a rational, utilitarian and straightforward way, which, I admit, is not my forte.

Quick: work twice as hard before the movers show up. One more box, where's the scotch tape? Sweep the corner - there, all the heaped-up dust, and the crumpled papers stuck behind the dresser. The only upside of manual work is that you don't think about anything else. It lets me forget the fact that I've just had a divorce, that I have no more money and that I haven't been able to write a single sentence for months, which is annoying for a writer. The worst thing is that I don't know what's worse: to draw a line under my past life, or to feel unsuccessful and useless, like a pan without a handle.

Writer's block sounds a bit clichéd, but an idle writer is as unhappy as a child who's been deprived of dessert. There's only one cure, apparently - to write: absolutely anything at all, but write. List names of cheeses, for example. *Banon, bleu de Gex Haut-Jura, bleu des Causses, fourme de Montbrison, mâconnais, pélardon, vacherin du Haut-Doubs, valençay...*My mouth waters. I realize I'm hungry. The problem with moves is that you always end up neglecting the food chain.

The doorbell rings. It can't be a neighbor; people don't talk to each other in upper-class neighborhoods. When I walk down the street,

7

no one says hello, and I say hello to no one. Maybe it's because I live in the nicest house on the street. It is rounded in form, with curved stained glass windows reaching for the sky; the bourgeois who built it at the turn of the 20th century didn't do things by halves. There's no denying it, these people had a sense of style.

I look like a slob. If it's the mailman, he'll mistake me for the cleaning lady. "I have a package for Mr. or Mrs. Zed, can you sign for them?" Too bad, I won't have to play the maid, because on my doorstep is a friend, a journalist I met at the Book Fair a few years ago. He was presenting a politically charged book about the left; for every book that he sold, I sold 10. A writer is often envious of the success of others, but he was generous enough not to hold it against me. Joachim is simply dropping by unannounced to say hello. There's someone with him, probably a guest he doesn't know what to do with; guests are like fish, they stink after three days.

"This is Marco, he's come from Turin to give a conference," he says, adding: "He's a well-known activist."

The way he pronounces the word, I understand that an activist is a militant twice over; an activist counts double, as in Scrabble. Is his comrade Che's natural son?

Joachim says to Marco: "Corinne is French and a writer; she published a book on Stendhal - you know, the author of *The Red and the Black*. It's called *Stendhal, Libertine Biography*."

I let them in. The activist is very, very attractive. That's putting it mildly. His yellow ochre eyes, the color of a sophisticated cocktail, capture mine without looking away. He has a slender and supple, plant-like body, and the precise gestures of someone who has a sense of belonging everywhere. He has the true beauty of a worker, like the ones who worked in my Dad's business when I was young.

He's bald, which gives him a bit of a mobster look. Not

unattractive. Note: he's a young bald guy, meaning he shaves his head, unlike old bald guys, who gather the little hair they have left into a ponytail, and *really old* bald guys, who stretch a strand of hair over the crown of their heads. His clean-shaven head is shaped like an electric light bulb, the kind that fell victim to sustainable development. Too much heat, not enough light – or the other way around, it doesn't matter. Anyway, he has an amazingly natural, rough, and mineral density.

The Italian looks around. He whistles with admiration and a touch of irony, which I don't notice right away. It's time to give him a history lesson.

"This is a house in the art nouveau architectural style conceived at the end of the 19th century. It's a style whose colors and shapes are inspired by the plant and animal worlds and... I'm an intellectual above all. I could have been a teacher, if that profession wasn't so socially undervalued."

He interrupts me sharply. He speaks perfect French.

"We could house ten Syrians at your place."

His statements sound absolute and compelling, as if they were vested with the authority of the KGB. He has a kind of swagger, as he has to win no matter what. I don't care about Syrians. I don't like lectures. This is my home and I do what I want.

I snap back: "This is what's called an *hôtel de maître* in Belgium. But there's only a mistress here, no master."

"How many rooms in your 'hôtel de maîtresse?'"

"So many that it would be petty to count them. No need for requisitioning, comrade, I'm leaving, I've spent all the money which I won with my last book. And I cleaned up before leaving."

"Did you learn cleaning at night school?" he asks, jokingly. He has a slicing voice, like steel marbles rolling across a pool of oil.

"I even know how to change the vacuum cleaner bag. And the filter!"

When I have to, I face up to things. I'm a *warrior*, though it may not seem like it.

"It's to your credit - or not, depending on how you look at it."

He's well spoken for a commoner, which is what my very bourgeois grandmother would have said. I take a shot at him:

"Not sure you'd succeed."

It's a challenge. Will he take it up? Statistics speak for themselves; men never vacuum, so changing the bag... A piece of cake, people say, an expression that means nothing: it took me some time to do it. The instructions helped. "Open the vacuum cleaner's valve by pressing on the corresponding button. Gently remove the bag filled with dust. Slide in the new bag along the racks until it is locked in. Close the cap."

Hands stuffed in his pockets, Marco doesn't make the slightest move to take the appliance.

I heat water in the microwave and serve coffee to the two men. That's all that's left in the kitchen: the oven, Nescafé, and two chipped cups. I insist:

"So, what about that vacuum cleaner?"

Joachim follows our little verbal duel like he would a game of Ping-Pong.

Marco quietly replies:

"I'm not your houseboy."

He takes off his jacket and I notice that his T-shirt is inscribed with the words "Working-Class Hero". He has a dragon tattooed on his right arm.

"Nice to meet you, comrade-hero. Welcome to Brussels."

"I already know the city. I once robbed a bank on Avenue Louise," he says calmly.

At this point, I must say, I'm blown away. Is he serious?

"Are you shocked?" he asks hopefully, puckering up.

It's better to stay in joking mode.

"How many class enemies killed?"

"None. It was the work of a professional."

"And what happened to the loot?"

"You mean the revolutionary tax? Struggles have to be funded..." he says, dodging the question with a shrug of the shoulder.

The boxes are waiting for me; I escort my visitors to the door. I ask the Italian:

"Where did you learn French?"

"In prison," he replies simply.

I'm dumbfounded. At the same time, the Berlitz language method is so unoriginal.

On the doorstep, Marco says with a tone of false formality:

"Goodbye, Madame."

"Goodbye, comrade."

Then he bends over; I see the glint of his sparkling eyes get close to me. I'm hypnotized; for a split second, I ask myself: "What does he want from me?" Then he interrupts the eye contact, stands still and says:

"I hope we see each other before 2017."

"Why 2017?"

He looks up in despair and raises his hands towards the agrestic mosaic that gracefully adorns the ceiling.

"Madame is not aware? We have a date in 2017."

What is he talking about?

I pretend to be a very busy businesswoman:

"Really? You and I? I don't understand... My personal assistant didn't tell me anything... My diary is already full...

He makes a *toot-toot* sound:

"Next year, the Russian revolution will be a hundred years old. It's something to celebrate properly, no?"

Properly? Is that a threat? Joachim gives me a friendly wink and the two men disappear down the street. Brussels is dripping with rain like a sponge soaked in water.

I shut the heavy double door behind me, destabilized by the atmosphere of innuendo and game playing generated by the stranger.

I'm discombobulated. The moment I had with the Italian haunts me, like an ultra-spicy dish whose taste stays in the mouth for a long time. He's very different from the cultural bourgeoisie to which I'm used to - kind, trendy, funny, but never crazy, strange or restless. Their lives are subdued, their views cautious. The only problem: they're *average*. They're like flavorless cheeses, closer to Dutch Gouda than to one of those sweaty blue French varieties stuffed with maggots. Their emotions are measured out in minimal doses that they never exceed. They never pronounce the word "hate;" it's too vulgar. They never lose control, never have a cat fight with people who don't think like them, never talk politics at the table. They don't know what they're losing; it's very stimulating. Judging by my childhood memories, it transforms any family meal into an out-and-out battle. Basically, if we argue, it's because we like each other.

The movers have removed the furniture. I've kept a small travel bag and my laptop computer close at hand. It's unlikely that he'll be listed in *Who's Who*, so I Google the Italian's name. The photo on his Wikipedia page shows a serious face with an enigmatic look. "Marco Di Giacopo is an Italian far-left figure. He was a member of the Communist Party Combatants cells, implicated in the destruction of buildings - NATO's in particular. He was sentenced to five years in prison. He received death threats on several occasions. This intellectual regularly takes part in debates in Italy and abroad."

Marco rocks. If there was a chair left in the house, I would collapse in it.

I'm overtaken by a flurry of questions, of the kind I never asked myself. How does one put together an explosive device? And set it off? How do you measure and manipulate TNT? What do you feel in the moment of the explosion? Fear or a kind of inexplicable jubilation? Do things happen as they do in the final scene of Antonioni's film, *Zabriskie Point,* where a villa is destroyed by a bomb in the name of the fight against consumer society? A burst of fire, raining debris, the music of Pink Floyd: a whole era. Though the film's message is clear, it's a shame about the house, a beautiful building with such perfect architectural lines – just the kind of place I'd like to live in when I have money again. Admittedly, I'm poor at the moment, but I know that this unpleasant state of affairs is only temporary. Poor for a day, rich forever. Poverty for me is a mere navigational error, as if I'd taken the wrong train. I'm going to reinvent myself; it's written in the stars.

Marco has scribbled his email address on a piece of newspaper. I'm dying to write to him. For fun? To continue the verbal duel? Out of defiance? To see if he'll reply? To know whether I can seduce him? Impossible to know, and that's what's interesting about it. I make up my mind. After all, only the petit bourgeois abide by rules. The upper middle class have absolutely none, and couldn't care less about what we think of them. I write the following message: "Marco, I'm coming to Turin soon for a literary reading. I would love for us to meet. What if we got together and tried to foment class struggle?" In reality, I have no reason to go to Turin. I add a left-wing touch to my message: "As far as writing is concerned, I could use your advice: I'm looking at producing more political and politically motivated texts." I haven't decided what kind yet: straight activist texts are such a deadly bore. Finally, I mention my new address in Molenbeek. A magic wand to *become less bourgeois* in his eyes.

Because migrating to this neighborhood of Brussels proves that I have slid down the social ladder. A tangle of gloomy red brick houses, concrete blocks and seedy canals: no one goes there. At least, no one I know. Apparently, the commune has been attracting tourists since the Brussels attacks; no-go-zone tourism is doing very well. Visiting places of urban dysfunction, industrial wastelands and other terrorism breeding grounds: expect a big frisson.

Not for me, thank you. Of course, some well-to-do urbanites live here. They're bourgeois-bohemians, those ambivalent people who are torn between gentrification and woolly principles. The kind of people who think that class warfare is dissolvable in social diversity, conviviality and Neighbors' Day. They play the gentrification game and the wonderful discovery of working-class neighborhoods. Me, the day I have money again, I have every intention of living in a nice area, with well-kept streets, welcoming cafés, and butchers where even the leg of lamb is dressed up. In short, a bourgeois neighborhood. Up-and-coming areas are not my cup of tea; I don't have the time to wait for them to *arrive*.

Hoping for an answer from Marco, I spend hours in front of my computer. Time coagulates, turns into a thick gruel. I'm pathetic. But I'm finally living life to the fullest: the sheer immensity of the challenges to overcome, the dark uncertainty of the event. And funny sounds in my stomach. MDG... I call him by his initials, because masters of the universe such as JFK or DSK are entitled to be recognized by their initials, so it's only fair that others should be as well. Besides, initials are a way of distancing myself from him, of keeping cool. If I pronounced his name, a boiling liquid would spread in my arteries: too risky.

He writes to me, finally. It's a good thing, because I was practically choking, and I breathe as if I was finally thrown into a chamber filled with pure, mild oxygen. The message leaps on my screen. "I'll see you with pleasure in Italy: accept a kiss from me, dearest." He's taken the bait. I'm on cloud nine. I'm a soldier who has broken through enemy territory with his finest artillery. Then I'm gripped by doubt: Dearest... Maybe he thinks I'm too expensive for him. Well, a woman is never too rich or too slim, as Wallis Simpson, the Duchess of Windsor, used to say.

How can I attract his attention? The truth is that, as far as seduction is concerned, beauty is the only currency that counts. I begin with an inventory of my looks, because the material aspect of things is the most important. a) I have blue eyes. All the better. Even if blue is the color of conservatives, it's hard to seduce with red eyes. b) I'm blonde. As everybody knows, men are attracted to blondes like syrup to a pancake: Fidel Castro, his Romeo y Julieta cigar stuck between his yellowing teeth, was a blonde addict. c) I'm pretty. I deserve no credit, because rich people are often beautiful; at least, that's what you read in surveys by researchers who've run out of controversial subjects. Anyway, with my good looks, I tick all the boxes: it should be easy to seduce him. I will eat him alive.

Mind you... A blonde with fine features corresponds more to the image of the fairy than to that of the *pétroleuse*. Fairness is so associated with calm and serenity that I ask myself: were there any revolutionaries with fair hair? Can you plant bombs after getting highlights? To find out more on the issue, I search among progressive heroines, activists. Oh yes, Jane Fonda, even if that ardent feminist who fought against the Vietnam war and for civil rights made the dubious choice of switching to fitness and aerobics afterwards. Only, is she a real blonde? You can only get a supermodel-blonde look at the finest hair colorists, which are also the most expensive, so haloed with so much gold, so much for revolution!

In a word, I have some tricks up my sleeve, but the moral aspect is problematic. I grew up in the '80s, a decade as odorless and colorless as insipid tofu, which permeated all the decades that followed. I never said no. I never campaigned. I never went on a hunger strike. I never even *contemplated* going on a hunger strike. I had a disenchanted youth. Despising Margaret Thatcher and George W. Bush on a couch while eating fat-free potato chips is not enough to buy back class consciousness. I should have fought in a South American guerilla group instead of wallowing in boredom in Paris with people who were in the vanguard of the past.

Until recently, I quietly assumed this egocentricity, worthy of a goddess of antiquity. But now... My bourgeois attitude has gone up in flames, like rum on a flambéed banana. I can't picture MDG with a beauty who submits to the laws of the market. He can only be interested in amazons of the uprising, in Spartacuses wearing skirts, in women that went around brandishing heads on a stick. Women who, in theory, are very far from my ideological spectrum...

But I will become left-wing. That's good, being left-wing is cool, Prada has a feast at the Communist Party headquarters, Sciences Po students voted in large numbers for Mélenchon, while Mathieu Pigasse, the *enfant terrible* of finance, poses as an anti-bourgeois. The "sons of" wear hip- hugging jeans and pretend to have a slight pseudo-populist accent. Meanwhile, Balenciaga sells a purse that's a copy of the famous Ikea blue bag: one costs 1,695 euros, the other, 80 cents. Bourgeois who act rich are history. They prefer to act poor; it's so much more interesting.

Being left-wing is just one step. I'm ready for action, I will go all the way. The problem is that I'm very clumsy - although I can open a bottle of champagne in less than 10 seconds. Me, plant a bomb? Pure and simple science fiction. The TV remote control, with its 56 buttons, is too complicated for me, so what do you expect me to do with a detonator? Much to my regret, I will have to make do with non-violent actions. If necessary, and as a show of good faith, I can provide a medical certificate. (I have known the famous Professor T. since I was little; he was a friend of my parents.)

Having two left hands won't stop me from protesting. I will put up posters at night; I will cover the walls with graffiti; I will glare at the CRS. I will go where the people revolt, rebel, run riot, and rise up. Fists clenched and tits in battle, I'll look pretty on a barricade, I'll be the *re-belle* on an anti-Vinci tractor. I will break my chains, sweep away the past and reach for the sky. My life will be exciting. It will be nothing but a long Night of August 4th.

What's great is that the left is like an open bar. You can choose to join the Caterpillar workers in Gosselies, the strikers of the Orangina bottling plant in La Courneuve, the German post office workers, or the Vueling flight attendants. Or occupy the Gràcia district in Barcelona with an anarchist collective. Or even use your body to block the construction of the Notre-Dame-des-Landes airport, the Welzow German mine, and the Lyon-Turin high-speed train. I'm tempted by everything, as when I look over the menu of a gourmet restaurant.

As I await to tip over the banquet table of capitalism, what am I going to eat now that I have moved to Molenbeek? I look out the Velux roof window, named after that Danish company that revolutionized the skylight. There must be a seedy bar further away, but I prefer not to run the risk of food poisoning. A smell of grease wafts through the apartment; it's coming from the hallway - more specifically, from the neighbor. I go and knock on his door. A flat-faced giant opens the door.

"Hello. I'm your new neighbor."

"Welcome! You'll like it here; it's a nice neighborhood."

"Can I ask you to kindly open your window? The smell of cooking is drifting into my home."

He stares at me, dumbstruck.

"But French fries smell good! Would you like some?"

I'm tempted to accept, as I'm hungry, but the smell drives me away.

Night falls; in the streets, the food shops look gloomy with their police-station lighting. I sound as if I know what I'm talking about; it's actually rare for people from my social background to be taken into custody. And when they are, they have a cell all to themselves, which is cheating. Prison is only for the poor, a bit like welfare benefits and sugary sodas.

Nonetheless, I've been doing some research by watching the footage of the arrest of Dominique Strauss-Kahn (DSK) and his incarceration on Rikers Island. An exhilarating spectacle for millions of viewers, the ones on the left as well as the ones on the right. On the left: 'Crack down on the managing director of the IMF, an institution that sucks the blood of the poor!' On the right: 'This socialist caught with his hands in the cookie jar got what he deserved!' To me, DSK is nothing but a vulgar nouveau riche guy who wears flashy watches. And who eats too much, which is truly unforgivable.

Anyway, my cultural acclimatization in Molenbeek will be difficult. I feel like I've crossed a time zone, even though I'm only three kilometers away from my old neighborhood. A collision of worlds. Thankfully, while emptying a box, I find a small can of homemade Pâté des Landes stuffed with foie gras. I polish it off and savor it with my fingers, which at least doubles the pleasure.

I Skype with my best friend Edouard, who lives in the States. He never fails to give me useful advice which he doesn't really believe in and which I don't follow. What's useful is unromantic. He's the only person who will accept to answer my unsettling questions without making any comments.

"Edouard, I want to ask you something. What does being left-wing mean to you?"

He pauses to think.

"Easy. It is being naive, big spender and hypocritical. Whereas to be right-wing is being brutal and intolerant. There is also a question of lifestyle. It's relying on all of Ken Loach's movies...eating merguez sausages in the rain at the Communist Party's annual Fête de L'Humanité gathering... wearing a *keffiyeh,* even if it's hard to match with normal clothes..."

"That's it?"

"Um... Adopting obsolete values, solidarity, generosity...joining 'Together,' even it includes a lot of assholes...writing about boring subjects...Oh, it's also voting for Philippe Poutou, a factory worker. Who will never be elected."

"Voting, are you sure? I thought elections were a con aimed exclusively at suckers?"

We gaze at each other from one screen to another, perplexed.

I have a feeling it will be a hell of a paradigm change, as hard as going from fast food to slow food. It will be a palace revolution.

Edouard is right to raise the problem of writing. I can't carry on writing entertaining books only to alienate the reader from genuine concerns and difficult struggles. A book has to be an express train charging into the future, not a slow train where you quietly snack while enjoying the scenery. As of today, *la vie en rouge* will come before *la vie en rose.* I will write books rooted in everyday life in its most tangible sense: hardcore reality, guaranteed non-fiction. My pen will be at the service of hard topics, the social divide, the tough neighborhoods, solidarity, poor housing...

It's time to bid farewell to Stendhal – the intense determination he brings to the pursuit of happiness is so trivial.

The reader will be bored to death? Too bad, being left-wing is something you have to work for.

I will overwhelm the media with beefy opinion columns to

explain what's useful to mankind. As a true Jedi knight resisting the Evil Empire, my first issue will be TAFTA. If this treaty is signed, chicken washed in chlorine, hormone-fed beef and GMOs will burst onto the European market. A gastronomical horror. Hold it right there: the gustatory red line shall not be crossed; I shall block it with my pen.

To develop a credible standing as a left-wing intellectual, it's essential to undertake theoretical work. Inevitably an essay on the Russian revolution since Marco said it; we need to deal with it properly. October 1917 is a fine, potent subject. I'm going to make a splash with this big idea : the past is the future. A little time-related bomb. This book will give me real legitimacy. The back cover will announce, to great applause: "Shunning all taboos, the author exorcizes her old demons, and wholeheartedly embraces this phantom that haunts the West: revolution." Powerful. I already imagine myself striking a pose and uttering definitive statements: "The Russian revolution, that major event... So revolution, yes, of course. Voilà .... voilà." When people no longer know what to say, they say voilà. So voilà, then.

I will shut Hélène Carrère d'Encausse up once and for all with my book. HCE, who turns 88 next summer, has been the queen of the Russian Intellectual Academy for at least 50 years. A peroxide wig glued to her head, she occupies the Russian terrain by fencing it with barbed wire, Berlin-Wall-style. She's planted her flag in the middle, like the red label on beef from the Charolais region, that treasure of Burgundian heritage. I envy her, of course, but not to the point of being jealous: she's right-wing. If you see her books in a bookstore, don't buy them. Wait for mine to come out: better here than there.

Without knowing it, Marco has pressed the button leading to a secret corridor, that of my past. Because the revolution and I met a long time ago. When I was little, my father would describe it to me so I could fall asleep at night. Lenin, Trotsky and a few others floated around me. It was a strange lullaby, but then my father was born in 1917. He had embraced communism as a religion, like so many Jews during that period. He died in 1988, before the fall of the Berlin wall, before the last Communist, that man abandoned by history.

Even though I was immersed in communism, I'm not a sucker as far as I know. I am well aware that there's good and bad in communism. After a few years of glorious unrest and bold experiments, the Russian revolution took a turn for the worse. As the saying goes, it ended up devouring its own children. The glorious interlude ended in blood. Secret police, widespread surveillance, repression, deportation of entire populations...Yes, so what? Is that a reason to throw it up? A lot of things go down the drain, no? Two thirds of couples separate or divorce. Is that a reason not to fall in love?

I open a new file that I name "Red" on my computer. Red as in revolution, and as in love. I begin to write down a few sentences to get started, and realize that I've forgotten the basics. Marxism, it has to be said, was already a dead language when I was born, a bit like Latin and Greek. In the '80s, during the acutely Reaganite and Thatcherite years, it wasn't used by anyone, except my parents, survivors of a dead world. Only I used it, and even then reluctantly, at home: commodity fetishism, reification of human relationships. My classmates wouldn't have understood. I looked like the Marranos, those Jews from Spain who secretly continued to speak in Hebrew to avoid having problems.

If I want to make a grand entrance into Leftie-land, I have to refresh my linguistic skills. But where? We're no longer in the blessed days when the philosopher Louis Althusser introduced his students to the Chinese Cultural Revolution. Yet a Marxist university takes place every year in Waterloo, and here I am on a bus going through the mournful plain where Napoleon's armies were beaten to a pulp. If an episode of the infamous battle appears at the beginning of *The Charterhouse of Parma*, Stendhal's topology is so vague that this battle could just as easily have taken place in Ruritania as in the Brabantine plains.

The courses are given at a school, a utilitarian building situated in the open fields. I go straight up to the dormitory, a cost-effective form of accommodation that matches my financial means. It's a big room in the attic, on the fifth floor, which is usually used as a gym for the students, who are on vacation right now. Everyone sets up wherever they want. I love to call everyone "comrade".

I put down my things and run off. I pace up and down the corridor looking for my classroom and discover that among those who have registered, some are good-looking. Everyone knows that the best way to brush up on a language is through pillow talk. But the conferences are already starting. They focus on growth, the economic crisis, wealth distribution, and austerity policy... And, of course, the revolution. I cherry-pick the talking points and take notes. The development of productive forces, the change in production methods, constant capital vs. variable capital, private property, capital accumulation, use-value vs. exchange value...

I haven't forgotten my vocabulary entirely. It's like bike riding; you never forget it. On the way, I pick up this lovely activist quote that's worth sharing: "Capitalism wants to turn the human belly into the governing body of mankind and convert the mind into a commodity." A quote from Paul Vaillant-Couturier (PVC), writer, politician and Communist. It's food for thought for me, because the belly is quite simply the part of my body that monopolizes my thoughts the most.

Attending the courses, I begin to grasp the meaning of the word popular, an adjective that's essential to the left. Its use requires thought, because it has very different meanings: plebeian, sought after, renowned, ordinary, widespread, famous, democratic, well liked. I'm not popular (as in plebeian) but I would like to be popular (as in well liked), but I'm not sure I want to be popular (as in well known). Because fame smells like easy money, vulgar starlets, soccer and reality TV.

Readers, it's your turn now. Practical exercise: popular, meaning 1), 2) or 3): Disneyland, Tintin? And Call of Duty? Neon, Rosé wine, David Guetta, Karaoke? The May Day protest? (There, it's easy.)

At lunchtime, the catering reminds me of my college cafeteria. It's truly, truly bad, but I have no choice; the word "gourmet" doesn't exist in Russian. During the Soviet era, "gourmet" referred to food stores where there was very little room for the exaltation of taste. Yet Russian gastronomy is recognized worldwide, with its profusion of piroshky, borscht, pelmeni, and kulebyaka. By the way, what was Lenin's favorite dish - stuffed mushroom turnovers, stuffed cabbage, salt meat or beat soup? I wouldn't have the answer today, but I bet this aspect of his biography has been kept secret. For political reasons, of course: pleasures of the palate are upper-class sensual delights. Cubans, who practice more glasnost, unveiled that Fidel Castro feasted on turtle soup.

In Waterloo, the atmosphere is friendly. The university is a scene of great social diversity: factory workers, self-employed people, teachers, job seekers, pensioners, and students. As I socialize, I gather interesting data on Communist festivals. You eat best at that of Avante in Portugal (three stars), followed by the Fête de l'Humanité in France (two stars), and Manifiesta in Belgium (no stars). My deep-rooted fear of crowds is an obstacle: the constant pushing back of the dangerous classes separates me from the people. I jot down on my to-do list: seek treatment for my agoraphobia. (Hello, Professor T?)

After an evening washed down with a fine amber-colored craft beer, I go to bed. Maybe there's a good-looking Palestinian among my roommates. Because Palestinians are to leftists what the Viet Minh were to militants in the 1960s: highly symbolic. In protests, you rarely escape the words of a Palestinian poet, declaimed with the appropriate dose of pathos. It's easy to write a Palestinian poem: simply take the words "land," "homeland," "soldiers," "liberty," "tears," "people," "war," and toss them all together.

Unfortunately, the dormitory is empty; my roommates have stayed at the café to change the world, with Manu Chao as background music. Except one of them... In the semi-darkness, I watch a guy who's getting undressed. The pale, cold moon highlights his figure nicely. Who said communism wasn't glamorous? He has very dark hair, he's probably an immigrant, and offhand, he'll replace the Palestinian. I spotted him at the cafeteria from the quiet and measured way he served his food -I hate pigs.

Long live a love that avoids the social divide. At this point, I know that the PC (politically correct) reader is making a face. He prefers to glorify Albert Camus's *The Stranger*, the chilling story of a Frenchman who kills an Algerian for no reason: the bestselling book in France.

My roommate turns around and sees that I'm looking at him. I get up and very gently take off my brand new Che Guevara T-shirt. I'm naked underneath...I haven't shaved my legs, because to obsess over bodily hair reinforces the stereotype of the woman as object. My erotic boldness, exemplified by this mini-Cuban striptease, delivers results: he offers me his hand; the way is open for every audacious move. We hide under his camping duvet and cavort with blissful voracity. He bites my ear; he's hot, and smells like a bread roll straight out of the oven. As his full lips grab mine, I go on a reconnaissance mission, and notice that he's circumcised. Marx was too, just like Trotsky, Zinoviev, Kamenev and quite a few others. But to go as far as defining circumcision as a leftist thing would be a case of historical revisionism.

It's time to pick the fruits of the night. I feel like making love like Lady Chatterley, this aristocrat who has an affair with the gamekeeper. With a clever wave of the hand, I cover his passion fruit with rubber icing. Then I hold him down under me, my legs on either side of the floor mat: a slow and structured ride. I'm the one who sets the pace, forward backward, forward backward, with a slight right-left rotation. It feels like I'm riding my favorite horse, a thoroughbred named Aramis. It's a little too hot, and to calm things down, I think of Leningrad in the snow.

We merge in the proper way, meaning my way. I'm the one who sets the pace; I'm the Great Leader. The missionary position, as the name suggests, merely seeks to control me, and colonial times have passed. I ascend to heaven while asking myself whether there is a paradise for Communists. Until now, for me, paradise was full board at Paul Bocuse, but I chose the wrong runway. I must have taken the one on the right instead of taking the one on the left.

And what if we did it again?

He leaves the next day, which will stop me from having to ask myself whether I'm in love with him. One night is too short to crystallize our relationship. So much the better: we're so stupid when we're in love, so romantic, stupid and starry-eyed... We get stuck in sentimentality. I go back to bed without saying a word, and fall asleep instantly, like a faucet that's been turned off. In addition to my intellectual skills, I'm inherently robust.

Yes, reader, it's already the end of what Italians call a *romanzetto*, a brief, unimportant romance.

I don't know his name; goodbye, Mr. No Name.

Turin, February 2016: the main course

Finally, finally, it's time for my date with Marco. These past weeks, a pair of naked lovers got inside my head, in a plastic bubble, covered in artificial snow. I found a reason to go to Turin: I have asked to be invited to the Stendhal Encounters, which take place every year on the sidelines of Turin's book fair. My Italian publisher is delighted, it will help boost sales, she figures. It must be said that I enjoy a *Stendhalian* aura, thanks to my *Stendhal, Libertine Biography*, where the reader (and especially the female reader) takes the writer to bed (Stendhal was ugly, with a big potato-shaped face, but when the lights are out, all cats are grey.) As the enthusiastic press wrote upon its release, "Nimble and well documented, this surprise bestseller unveils all the keys of the writer's erotic universe, exploring the trails of the heart and pleasure."

Naturally, I regret not being able to live my romantic Revolution in Venice, a much more romantic city than Turin, with its domes, its steeples and its palaces streaming with gold. The living proof? A night train, the *Stendhal*, connects Paris to Venice. With a twinge of regret, I abandon *La Serenissima* to the aesthetes, and to Philippe Sollers, the leader of that circle of French intellectuals who reconfigured Marxism and turned it ... into Chinese.

From above, Turin isn't an appetizing place. Its geometric layout reminds me of the inside of a waffle iron. The city initially offers extended views of its parallel streets, punctuated with neat symmetrical squares. Beneath this austere exterior, however, it hides an epicurean taste for good food and fine wines. Turin is an obligatory stop for its gastronomy. In culinary terms, my stay gets off to a great start. I've scraped together every last penny; I'll be able to treat myself to a few gourmet follies.

Note: I'm not just a belly. I'm aware that this city is the birthplace of struggles and, as such, a leftist landmark. From the spring to the autumn of 1969, starting from the famous Fiat factory, the workers' revolt inflamed Italy and let out its cry of war against the bourgeoisie: *We want everything.* It's the "Hot Autumn," the highlight of the revolutionary wave rippling across the Italian peninsula during the 1970s.

I'm staying at the Down Plaza, a business hotel. Very business-oriented, it's equipped with four conference rooms for which I have no use. The functional décor of my room is highlighted by a view of the Empire State Building hanging above the headboard. I barely look at it before jumping into a cab. It's noon. The zucchini flowers stuffed with ricotta cheese, Piedmont veal, saffron risotto, and pan-fried cassoeula will get cold. No need for company, I don't like to be watched while I'm eating. I'm not pretty when I eat. What matters is that I'm going to enjoy a three-star-Michelin day.

Marco is waiting for me in the early afternoon on Piazza San Carlo, Turin's baroque square. I've finished eating, and have suitably honored Italian gastronomy. How wonderful, la cassoeula... A dish based on *verza* (kale), rind, sausage and pork meat, to which you add carrots, celery, onion and butter. The dish gives off its full autumnal flavor when it's accompanied by cornmeal polenta. That's what's called real cuisine, the kind that comes from the guts and smells of fragrant casseroles handled with love. I emptied my plate with a militant fervor: a blast, a surge, the kind of experience where you come out literally seared. And for dessert, a *zabaglione*, a frothing delight: a mix of egg yolk, sugar and Marsala wine enough to make you faint. I've absorbed enough calories to feed an African village.

Feeling heavy from the digestion, I have to stop on the street corner to pump air like a fish out of water. The cold, which weighs on everything like a lid, extracts the oxygen in the air the way you'd swallow a sorbet. A wind that's sharp as a knife carves into the winter day. Marco doesn't seem to be cold, he's standing on the curb, his thumbs in his jean pockets. With his studied bad-boy pose, his slim torso and his brown leather jacket, he could almost be modeling for a magazine – his "Fight the rich" sweater gives him a pretty attractive punk look.

I'm looking my best today, physically: it takes a ripe piece of cheese to catch the mouse. A frumpy bourgeois woman has no charm in the eyes of a man, leftist or not. It wasn't easy turning myself into a princess, I only try to make myself beautiful when I want to seduce. The tangle of shapes, colors and styles puzzled me at first. It must be said that what's called keeping up with fashion is as interesting for me as going on a package tour, or buying an off-plan house in a housing development. It's very simple: you either do fashion like my great-great-grandmother Hedwig, arbiter of taste in the interwar years – or you leave it to the little people, those who imitate the upper classes.

I deploy all my feminine artillery by following *Vanity Fair's* advice. Expensive preparations have reduced me to being like an enticing table set for the male libido, like a well-cooked dish designed to make his mouth water. Under my coat, I'm wearing a very simple, well-cut little dress that's worth a fortune. For a lay person, it looks fresh out of a second-hand shop, with its scruffy-wrinkled-faded natural look. God bless female appearances, even if God doesn't exist.

My only reservation: if Marco takes it off, he'll notice that the satin lining, dotted with big yellow and orange pieces, is much too sophisticated to be inexpensive. When the time comes, I'll have to quickly curl it up in a ball and shove it under the bed. Under the bed... I'm getting ahead of myself, because I don't know whether the passage to sensual affection will be possible. Is that what Stendhal calls *"a love of the mind"*, meaning a nervous romance?

My underwear is 100% leftie-friendly. I've chosen the most ordinary, faded and timeless pair, with visible elastic waistbands. In short, a "Soviet" pair. It's for reasons of activism that I haven't bought sexy underwear; European underwear has been hit quite hard by globalization. The production of branded underwear and bras is almost entirely outsourced to Tunisia, Morocco, and China. No need to wrap my cute ass in a goody bag produced by the economically weak.

I feel his chestnut-colored eyes checking me out from top to bottom. I can tell he finds me elegant – maybe a little too much. Is he afraid of my pretty dress and its sophisticated fabric, which could be viewed as flag-bearers of the bourgeoisie and as the Trojan horses of capital? What if I've gone over the top? I feel exposed; what's revealed is not my body, but the money I spent to clothe it. I am crippled with the fear of not being attractive or good enough.

The heated exchange I was simultaneously expecting and fearing begins with kid gloves, immediately. He seeks my gaze like a sword, initiates the duel, and puts the boot in.

"And your Louboutin shoes, did you leave them at home, as a surprise gadget?"

The revolutionary has noticed that I'm wearing ballet flats, far from the improbable stilettos created by Christian Louboutin. Marco has heard of those famous sensually curved pumps with blood-red soles. The French designer has monopolized the color: what a scandal, that privatization. On my to-do list: launch an online petition on change.org so that individuals, the people, get back control.

"Pfft...Nouveau-riche footwear."

I should have thought twice before opening my mouth. That sentence was a tactical error. Only the bourgeois know the difference between the rich and the social climbers. The latter are vulgar, the women buy haute couture clothes that they don't know how to wear; the men show off their Rolex watches to prove that they have money. They snap their fingers at La Tour d'Argent or Fouquet's to call a waiter to their table. Real rich people have nothing to prove.

Angela Merkel is the perfect embodiment of this cultured bourgeoisie that scorns the vanities of the world. In German, it's called *Bildungsbürgertum*. A single word is enough to summarize that phrase, proof of the German language's extraordinary capacity for synthesis. No surprise if Marx was German. Merkel wears a watch that isn't even worth 100 euros: neither expensive nor flashy, it's just right. Through the simplicity of her clothes and her lifestyle, which verge on boredom, she turns off the French, those frivolous people who enjoy showing off.

Marco doesn't grasp these subtleties, and snaps back:

"Excuse me, I haven't mastered the upper-class dress code."

I have therefore made two mistakes, one sartorial and the other linguistic. The combination of these two disasters is a bit like mixing a poor rosé wine with exotic fruit syrup.

Quick, make it right to avoid a fashion drama.

"Charlotte Corday's shoes would be more appropriate."

The woman who murdered Marat in his bathtub in 1793 is the first female terrorist in French history. What shoes did Charlotte, also a pretty girl, wear on the day of the attack? (All we know is that at the time, the shoes were exactly identical: there was neither a right nor a left foot. I say that in passing to enhance the reader's general knowledge, even though it really doesn't matter.)

"You're thinking of shoes for warrior women?"

"Exactly!"

This time, his eyes sparkle. Phew, I'm saved; I've managed to inject a touch of *disinvoltura* into the discussion. A beautiful smile, small discreet gestures to tame my strands of hair without really trying, I leisurely walk by his side. I have no idea where we're going. The passersby are too uninteresting to have faces. Marco has his hands in his pockets and his shoulders slightly hunched because of the wind. It occurs to me that my partner is living under a death threat, and that anything can happen, which adds even more piquant to our walk.

"What's on your program in Turin?" he asks me.

"In the late afternoon, I'm participating in the Stendhal Encounters."

"At the Lingotto? That factory that's been turned into an arts center, what a shame...All the memories of the working class are lost."

"Yes... At the same time, churches end up as discotheques, fish markets as co-working places, brothels as nurseries...The post-industrial economy is like that."

My somewhat relativistic remark annoys him.

"Factories are part of the heritage," he insists.

If only he knew how right he was. My father owned two of them.

Thankfully, he changes the subject.

"What are you going to talk about?"

"I'll touch on the revolutionary Stendhal. That's how Maxim Gorky characterized Stendhal."

I guess Maxim Gorky, the Russian writer who founded the socialist realist literary style and who was politically active among the Bolshevik revolutionaries, knew what he was talking about. Actually, I don't know anything about it, and am about to improvise on something far more frivolous. My presentation is called "Stendhal, the European tour of a gourmet." Enough to make the audiences' mouths water.

"Stendhal, a revolutionary? I'm dubious. Let's not forget that he was a reference point for your French writer, Drieu-la-Rochelle," he hits back.

There's a hint of aggressiveness in the "your." Is it an anti-fascist reaction to Drieu-la-Rochelle, that indefensible anti-Semitic writer? Or do I sense a pinch of anti-French sentiment?

"Drieu doesn't belong to me. Nor does France. There are only two nations: the exploiters and the exploited," I say, cutting him short. "The idea of the homeland is a stupid idea."

I'm perfect. I could get a part in that Jean-Luc Godard (JLG) movie *La Chinoise*, where young bourgeois proclaim their love for Mao.

"A stupid idea for those who have one," he observes. "That's what Jean Genet used to say. I'm well placed to talk about it; I'm a pariah in my own country..."

What did he expect, after his bomb-making exploits? To be welcomed with champagne and a selection of savory appetizers? But then I like men of culture. Not like traders, golden boys, bankers in the City, all those who only speak of profitability, return on investment (ROI) and profit. Those who run on treadmills as they watch the stock-market prices, those modern-day barbarians, the ruin of the western soul.

With Marco, it will be different. We'll talk for hours. From

Stendhal to Marx, evenly, fifty-fifty. Marxism's illuminations, Stalinism's betrayals, and the thrills of *Stendhalism.* In the beginning, love is an all-you-can eat buffet; then you need to spice it up to keep a little appetite - first physical, then metaphysical. Oh, love, that yummy mix of games of the tongue and games of the mind...

I speak to him of Marcel Proust, that fan of "one of those short plump cakes called Petites Madeleines that look like they were moulded in a scallop's grooved valve." Here his face gets into a twist, Proust is not his kind of literary sustenance. That awful bourgeois loved duchesses and cathedrals, and slept with the driver. Are we heading towards a war of taste? The response is not long in coming. "Proust is *pre-fascist*," claims Marco. Never heard that word. *Pre-fascist* must mean decadent and despicable. And *post-fascist* would mean what? Let me guess. Surely, 1945, the bourgeoisie in disarray, the establishment of social security, company nationalizations... *Post-fascist*, translation: cool, great, wicked.

He takes me to a friend's trattoria near Via Po. The owner welcomes us with a smile that reveals a gleaming golden tooth. "The Calabrian and I met in prison," says Marco: so much more original than any Rotary Club. We climb the stairs to a small deserted room upstairs.

"Are you hungry?"

"No. I had a sandwich when I got to the airport, I have no more room for pasta."

No need to mention the place where I ate lunch. The rebel's DNA is incompatible with costly feasts.

"You know, the food is good here. You can have the *pasta alla carbonara.* The members of a secret utopian society, the Carbonari, invented it. It's a recipe for people chased by the police who were forced to cook fast with simple things; they were always on their toes. I too make it well," he adds with a sly grin. I can't believe it.

"You really know how to cook?"

That makes up for the running away from the vacuum cleaner.

"I'll invite you...In the meantime, I'll have a *finanziera*, a traditional Piedmontese recipe made with cockscomb," he says rolling the 'r' of *finanziera*.

This dish is awesome. To eat it is to cross a gourmet's Rubicon. At the Oral Shock Syndrome (OSS) award, not yet recorded in the fifth edition of the Diagnostic and Statistical Manual of Mental Disorders, or DSM-5. (I know what this is, I had a discussion about it with Professor T.)

"Do you know where the name comes from? *Finanziera* was the favorite dish of merchants at the Turin Stock Exchange. The ones that weren't yet called traders," he explains greedily, delighted by this poke at the money world.

And for dessert? What's he going to have? Are there any left-wing desserts? A sugarcoated bomb perhaps?

As he eats, he talks about himself, his childhood in a poor milieu, his father, a Fiat factory worker. He's very proud of him and has no social inferiority complex. He's a one-man Proletarian Pride.

It's my turn to talk about myself. I should avoid telling him who my Dad was, avoid revealing the number of employees he had (many, far too many). It will be a secret as well kept as the Coca-Cola formula, stored in the back of a safe. There's no question of revealing the fact that my family is full of entrepreneurs and businessmen, that my genealogical tree is linked to the timeline of industrial France: it would ruin my romantic plans. I won't mention the fact that I'm the decadent product of the same triumphant society that also gave birth to a Debussy or a Monet. Builders, moneygrubbers or artists, those epicurean and cunning bourgeois know that the rosette of the Legion of Honor is mainly used for getting a last-minute restaurant table. Despite the crushing responsibility of having to govern a grouchy France, some people dream of occupying the Elysée: the presidential palace has what is unquestionably the best table in France, and its miraculous wine cellar contains the oldest vintages of a thousand Grands Crus.

A gap the size of a large tablecloth separates me from the person I'm speaking to: I'm *post*, he's *pre*.

The words float in my mouth. I look at my plate with the hope that the china will help me. Much to my relief, Marco calmly declares: "What's important is not people's origin, but what they do." I gratefully agree. Is it my fault if my father was a businessman and my mother a baroness? They hid it well, they didn't want to be prisoners of their privileges. Since noticeable money smells like stolen money, my parents had a tendency to hide it, sometimes to the extent of not spending it at all: better to be pitied than envied. Being an object of curiosity, even hate, living in a watertight survival ghetto? Oh no, never. They were twisted, and had all the tricks to look poorer than they actually were; the absence of status symbols allowed them to avoid being robbed on the street by petty criminals, and to ensure that no one was interested in them for their money. The good distance in relation to money, which is a sharpened form of snobbery, is to pretend to be broke. We think poverty is rigid and virtuous; in reality, that's sometimes the case with wealth.

I watch him eagerly gobble up his *finanziera*. Elbows on the table, I deliberately slouch, because my stiff manners might look awkward in this ordinary place. Meanwhile, he wipes the sauce on his plate with an attractive movement of the hand, right-left, right-left, then flips it all into the mouth. It's precisely at that point that I feel lifted past the shaky borders behind which the passions that eat out our heart are confined. Something bursts open in my bosom, like a chestnut freed from its peel.

We go out on the terrace to smoke a cigarette. I'm shivering in my luxury rag. The clouds haven't yet opened their belly and dumped snow, and I could drop dead in these Siberian temperatures. To get my mind off the goose bumps, I think very hard about the sunny balcony in *Vanina Vanini*, the Stendhal novel where an arrogant princess falls in love with a revolutionary. Except that right now, it's winter and there are no orange trees. Nor kisses. For the time being.

I slowly get closer to him. Our quivering, tensed-up bodies are almost touching. I feel his warm breath caressing my face. I drown myself in his eyes. I caress his shaven head with my hand. The feeling of touching my cousin Alix's hairless cat overtakes me, and I banish that nagging animal thought. I desire him with the urgent and compelling lust that a dieter would have for a Norwegian omelet. I fling myself at him like a starving jackal. In a French kiss, the man is supposed to do the honors, but I'm the one who goes on the offensive. As Lenin used to say, quoting Napoleon, "One jumps into the fray, then figures out what to do next." Our lips collide, our teeth rattle together, our tongues engage in a duel. I enter into him with my eyes closed, and mess up everything inside, a real oral attack.

His manliness caresses my groins. A blazing fire lights up inside me. Here I am as hot as a churros stand. Our legs get tangled up, and we stumble clumsily. My skin demands a revolution, its radiant cities and its soft alcoves. In this deserted space, with a cold wind blowing, I'm ready to offer myself like a feast of rum baba, whipped cream and langue-de-chat cookies.

And that's when the mechanism gets jammed. His lips turn all shy, his arms hold me less decisively; I feel that he's escaping me. Are my taste buds too laden with all the juices of Italian gastronomy? Is my passionate tongue too invasive?

The moment is gone. The mysterious alchemy of flavors and tastes didn't work. I wonder why. Maybe it's the fault of the Erbaluce di Caluso passito wine, with its fruity notes and mineral sensations culminating in a slightly bitter finish... Did that delicious Piedmontese wine affect my breath? Bitterness, that's the problem. And yet I didn't skimp on the "Vanilla Fresh Breath" spray. But it wasn't enough. I should have smeared my lips with the berry-flavored "Intimate Play," whose purpose is to enhance oral sex. Which means that it's more effective than a standard spray.

Unfortunately, there's no Lenin quote on food or kissing, and even less of one on the oral fiasco. The austere father of the October revolution warned: "The excesses of sex life are a sign of bourgeois degeneration." There's no danger of that happening in my case, and, believe me, I regret it.

We leave the terrace.

"A classy kiss that warms the heart," Marco soberly comments, before adding: "I have to leave, I work for a printing company. See you later. I'll call you," he says on the sidewalk.

Halfheartedly, I turn and walk away.

The Stendhal Encounters take place at the Lingotto, which means ingot in Italian. In the name of urban resilience, the factory has been converted into "the largest multi-purpose conference center in Europe." Meeting room, hotel, shopping mall and the inevitable art gallery (the Agnelli family's picture gallery) are all gathered together in one place. And, the icing on the cake, a heliport. Missing are the concept store garden and all sorts of pop-up stores to create a real mishmash of modernity.

This is Fiat's first production site, and its original design was inspired by Ford's Highland Park factory in Detroit. The factory played a major role in the Italian company's development, and has operated continuously since 1917. It's where the Fiat 500 was made, a kind of Western version of the Trabant. The raw materials were delivered on the ground floor and assembled on the assembly lines spread out across the various floors, which were accessed by an internal ramp. The finished cars arrived on the test track, on the roof. Once tested, the Fiats would go down two ramps. The raw materials entered from the bottom of the building, and the cars came out of the top... From bottom to top, not like the recommendations contained in the cleaning handbook.

Because of the security arrangements, I'm momentarily anxious before walking in. The crowd in the entrance is tight, as hard as a chilled cassoulet. The Lingotto is guarded like a safe. Since the terrorist attacks, book fairs are protected like Fort Knox. Inside, in the book fair's aisles, authors sit around little tables in front of piles of books. They wait for the customer. To keep up a front, some look at their fingernails, others tap on their smartphone. Tomorrow, it will be my turn to be a wallflower. What bothers me most is the prospect of having to get sustenance at the cafeteria, with its pale pasta and its greasy artichokes.

In the Incontri Stendhal room, the attendees are already seated. There are a lot of them. Is it because Italians love Stendhal as much as he loved them? Here's proof that feelings are always mutual, which is reassuring for me. But these pasta bellies, I'm sure, are especially attracted by the buffet, which concludes the debate.

Turin is the city where Henri Beyle, better known as Stendhal, lived in 1815. He had arrived in Italy a few years earlier, with Napoleon's troops. This country drove him "mad with joy." He was in love with a Milanese woman, Angela Pietragrua, "the perfect beauty." In Italy from 1814 to 1821, he met a woman he loved passionately, Matilde Viscontini. She resisted his advances and, ever since, Stendhal has been regarded as a prototype of the rejected suitor, the loser lover. He comforted himself with Italian cheese, *gorgonzola, mascarpone, pannerone*...Or the *stracchino delle valli orobiche* : produced with the milk of cows exhausted by seasonal migration, it leaves a sharp, intense taste in the mouth.

The conference obviously starts with clichés. The fair director's speech opens with the same old tune: in this uncertain world we live in, blah blah blah. Then he weaves together an Esperanto of platitudes on the book industry, that place of memory, that window on the world, which encourages coexistence and banishes intolerance. He stops short of saying that reading is a way of keeping people busy: when they read, they don't think of doing any harm. If only we could force them to read...

In an inspiring voice, the man with the bow tie details the multiple initiatives undertaken to rescue literature. He holds back from saying it, but it doesn't interest many people anymore. Tomorrow's writers will talk about technology, the global economy, and the computerized traffic of wealth. If the world has to end up in a single book, as prophesied by Mallarmé, it won't be a novel. It probably won't be a book either, but a simple file...

The great Stendhalian event can finally begin. The speakers follow one another. There's the pedagogue: "The question of children's education in *The Red and the Black*." The scholar: "A Stendhal portrait-a-clef in chapter II of *The Charterhouse of Parma.*" The literary: "Borrowed from the *Marriage of Figaro* in *Armance.*" The geographer: "Julien Sorel's itineraries in Turin." The self-important person who utters sentences expressing unequivocal truths, riddled with convoluted terms like intersubjectivity and metafiction, agent of impulsive representation.

While a female speaker makes revelations on "Stendhal and spinach" (the writer's favorite dish), I discreetly send a text to my friend Edouard. Given the time (it's 7 p.m. in Turin, 1 p.m. in New York), he's certainly having lunch in a crowded, noisy and expensive

- but macrobiotic - restaurant.

"I'm in Italy. I have designs on someone ... Should I pull out all the stops?" I love to tell him my life story. In matters of love, having a witness makes things even more spicy. His reply comes a few minutes later, and breaks my stride:

"Take it easy! No *furia francese!*"

Furia francese is that audacity that makes that you rush into danger by gambling with your life. Edouard knows me well.

So when Marco sends me a text to ask me whether I'm free in the evening, I don't reply. Play for time, keep waiting, act cold. (Is there a *Love for Beginners* handbook? With practical tips?) It's my turn to speak. The spinach speaker paved the way for me. Stendhal, that gourmet, discovered culinary specialties in a Europe he traveled through hurriedly in the course of his Napoleonic conquests. First as Cavalry Second Lieutenant, then as Quartermaster General of the Great Army, he eagerly tasted Russian borscht, Austrian *wienerschnitzels*, Italian pasta and German sauerkraut. The Stendhalian Europe, that of taste buds and fine dining, is much more flavorful than the Europe of technocrats and financial stability pacts.

Then, in a spectacular turn of events, I introduce a new element likely to stir up the audience: the writer actually didn't like sauerkraut. It's precisely at that point that I notice a silhouette at the back of the room... By Karl Marx's beard! It's Marco... Disaster. The topic of my conference is not what I had told him it was going to be. Will I sound convincing when I tell him that there is only one step from Karl Marx to Thierry Marx, the cook? And that this step is... *post-Marxist?* I wager that we have entered the post-truth era, that way of adapting the truth by riddling it with alternative facts and incoherent justifications...As soon as I finish my speech, I step down from the podium feeling as if my legs were stuck in molasses.

Exhausted by the tyranny of the material world, I trip and almost fall flat on my face. A clumsiness that goes unnoticed, as everyone gets up, and Marco disappears. Phew.

Chiara, my press attaché, shows me to the reception organized by the French embassy in honor of Stendhal and Stendhalians. Everyone rushes into the great hall. The organizers and the officials, with their understated elegance, contrast with a handful of blond, duck-lipped, post-Berlusconian bimbos. Academics have a rather indistinctive style; wearing any old thing, they try hard not to look either like business people or like their own students. Writers fade into the background: you can spot writers from the fact that you don't notice them. They're generally not very communicative; don't count on them to clown around or liven up the party. You can be sure that they're obsessing over small, unpleasant episodes that only concern them, and that they chew over like some kids do their own snot. (*My book didn't sell because a rotten cover was forced upon me. I didn't get a scholarship from the* National Center for Books *because of a maneuver by X, that bastard.*)

Here, you find the cream of the Stendhalian world: the people that surround me are insiders much more than I am, I who only ever wrote one book on Stendhal. They present themselves with spontaneity. I enjoy the spectacle, I notice the academic postures, the angle of the shoulder, the position of the arm, the inclination of the glass, and the painted-on smile.

Then my well-trained eye draws up an inventory of the buffet. The verdict is clear: undeserving. Dreary petits fours and greenish *verrines* (of guacamole?) Public institutions are on a diet, and the quality is suffering; soon, they'll impose dog biscuits and cheap sparkling wine.

Well, what did I tell you? Here they are serving a flat Prosecco that lacks the subtlety of champagne, its delicacy and finesse. And all the things that exalt the oral cavity and the nasal cavities, the touch of citrus, the note of ripe pear, the sensation of undergrowth, of berries, toasted bread or brioche...

Striking a tone suited for cocktail party encounters, I put on my usual act as the carefree and playful young woman. I look around for Marco. I see him about 20 meters away. He's making a splash; heads are turning in his direction.

Chiara whispers:

"Look, you see that guy over there? It's MDG, a leftist who placed a bomb in Italy."

I glance over, pretending to look detached:

"Oh yeah, I think I know him. His face looks familiar."

"Let's hope the ambassador doesn't see him, there's going to be a clash," says Chiara, worriedly.

"You know what Stendhal used to say? 'Only a prison sentence can distinguish a man. It's the only thing that cannot be bought.'"

As a true professional Stendhalian, I slip in a quote by the master at the appropriate time.

"But whose crazy idea was it to invite him?" asks Chiara.

I don't want to end up as collateral damage in a post-Cold War conflict. Discreetly abandoning my full glass, I disappear. In any case, I no longer believe in the evening's romantic potential. According to the buttered cat paradox, whatever gets off to a bad start rarely ends well: bread always falls on the buttered side.

I'm exhausted. I go back to the hotel. Alone in my room, I finally manage to breathe without feeling like I've swallowed a big object that's stuck in my lungs. Relieved, I slide under my duvet, a form of bedding whose global omnipresence is irrefutable proof of Scandinavian imperialism. I spread out on the sheet like butter on toasted bread and turn off the spectral light beaming from the ceiling.

To compensate for the day's frustrations, I would gladly watch a porn movie. It's the sexual equivalent of fast food, but it makes sense to fight stress with debauchery. I turn on the huge TV screen. The less people watch it (at least, people of my social background), the more enormous the screen is, as if in revenge. I look for the selection of movies offered by the hotel. At that very moment, I remember the startling words of a Soviet woman during one of the programs bringing together Russians and Americans in 1986: "There's no sex in the Soviet Union." Discouraged, I suspend my gesture and put down the remote control.

It's better to sensibly close my eyes and call on my imagination. I have enough food for thought to feed my fantasy machine. First, I replay the terrace scene, enjoying every second like when I was young and savored a coffee éclair, by making each bite last as long as possible. Then I picture myself in the air with Marco. We're flying over Red Square in a helicopter, a real raspberry pie sprinkled with sugar and topped with a multicolor hard candy. We get on the Baïkal-Amur Mainline (BAM), the 2nd Trans-Siberian railway, capable of crossing seven mountain ranges and traveling 4,232 kilometers. In the heart of the snow-whipped Taiga, I take his clothes off on a bearskin, near a smoking samovar, and our mouths work their way across each other's bodies.

None of these over-romantic dreams of a starry-eyed red girl are...popular. Should I feel guilty to be betraying the camp of the destitute? What do you dream of, female readers, when you're in love? Of a declaration of love under a Polyvinyl Chloride (PVC) veranda that's been marked down 50%? Of a stolen kiss in the supermarket cafeteria, in front of the chicken nuggets?

Then what are you doing nosing through this book? Don't justify yourself; you're still welcome. The duty of hospitality is a Communist duty.

New York, March 2016: the cheese course

A pale sun disappears behind the New York skyline. My sister is pottering around her open kitchen countertop, a symbol of conviviality and sharing. It's the key element of her cozy-chic loft, which has a pool table in the basement, a porter and a gym. It's a nice change from Molenbeek, and this is why I am here – Edouard charitably paid for my plane ticket. I have the impression of going from one world to another. But which is the dark side of the other?

The space, an aluminum ingot, is impeccable. It's too bad, because those who convert their kitchen into a temple of gastronomy, an atelier where one creates life, are often those who don't cook. In fact, my sister isn't one of those senior managers who believe in fooling around in the kitchen. She uses her oven to put away her dishes, not to cook; that says it all. She will surely force the unavoidable New York finger foods on us: pastrami sandwiches and bagels. Or, worse still, a combination of both: pastrami bagels.

Edouard, our mutual friend, opens the fridge and rummages inside, unsuccessfully, to find something edible. He only finds a piece of Camembert, which he nibbles on carelessly. In a black suit, meticulously shined (not by him) Italian shoes, and short hair, he's shaven with a straight razor by a master barber. His figure reveals a fitness enthusiast: the chocolate-bar-shaped abdominals are outlined under the white shirt, which is worn with a tie. The only touch of color: the red cardinal socks from Gammarelli, a Roman store renowned for its ecclesiastical outfits. The ultimate in elegant foot accessories.

His inconspicuous rich-guy look leads me to make an ironic remark.

"Edouard, what eccentricity! You could almost risk driving away the rich customers of your art gallery!"

He replies in the same tone. We love teasing each other.

"Yes, it's the revenge of pure color. I won't take any lessons in stylishness from the worst-dressed person in our entire class."

I accept; I wear second-hand clothes. I have chosen a kind of elegance through refusal, the look of absolutely no look at all. There's nothing flashier than brand new clothes, with sharp folds and the label still attached. My grandfather Alfred used to have his groom wear his boots before using them for the first time, to give them a patina, a story. A style.

"Even less from someone who wears *panini* as shoes," adds Edouard, half-ironic, half-sad.

He's referring to the large flat shoes with which I get around in Manhattan, where walking is an essential means of transportation. I charge back:

"I don't need to turn into a fashion victim to seduce the men I want."

My sister weighs in at the right time:

"At my business school, we spray-painted the dullest and ugliest coats with the campus colors. Anything to avoid boredom. Good thing you didn't go to a business school, Corinne."

Good thing, indeed.

My sister thinks she's funny, and tries hard to show that she had a rebellious youth. It's true that she spent a few years hanging out with a circle of precious, scornful and superficial girls. It was her way of standing up to her family, as money and showing off were not how we did things in the family. Now, she's ultra-conservative and looks like a Ralph Lauren commercial. She always wears makeup, and her hair is so flat, it looks like it's been ironed. (The opposite of mine, which is curly: the Babyliss hair straightener is just a bimbo gadget.) Her nails are impeccably filed and painted a vermillion color, and her teeth are extra-white.

She personifies social success, and her marriage is perfect: the man whom she chose looks like her. The rich marry each other, maybe because it is well known (although never expressed) that mixed marriage never work. She lives near Central Park, and one day, she will move far away from the low-lifes to a protected, remote area, preferably in a part of the world least affected by climate change, where the rich hastily build luxurious shelters. Because the rich man is paranoid and flees the masses. I'm the opposite, I run after them. And I'm not the first. The *établis,* those intellectuals originating from the bourgeoisie, fascinated by a working-class world they sanctified, decided after May '68 to go to work in a factory. The people were the Prince Charming of the Revolution. Meanwhile, Pasolini was interested in the *ragazzi* of Rome's inner city, and Marguerite Duras would drink bad wine in truck stops on the outskirts of Paris. Jean Genet, for his part, praised the Palestinian cause by glorifying its fighters: "the sparkle of the eyes, the voltage of the temples, the jubilation in their blood." (Note: 'Fedayeen' is a useful word in Scrabble, with the 'y' worth 10 points.)

Socio-economic differences feed sexual excitement, and Genet, who loved thugs, understood it well. What could be a more powerful aphrodisiac than the class divide? Unfortunately for my probably frigid sister, the underprivileged and the marginalized are not her type of beauty. In her living room is a very preppy photo of her husband and children. The latter have gone skiing in the Catskills for a few days. Good riddance.

Their absence allows me to take over the children's room - more specifically, to make my way through the heap of shredded toys and unidentifiable debris. Don't expect me to tidy up. What the hell is the cleaning woman doing? Twiddling her thumbs? It's obvious she's not doing her job properly. If I were a snitch, I would say something to her employers.

I don't know which jerk is trying to make us believe that tenderness is back in kids' rooms, and that a child is a carefree little blond-haired angel. What's more dreadful than walking on an abandoned Happy Meal toy in the middle of the night, an abandoned piece of Lego, or a Playmobil statuette, all cunningly lurking in the dark to laminate your foot? What's more intriguing than those so-called board games that seem destined not to create a community of players, but to be rendered unusable as soon as possible, and dismembered by harmful hands?

Here's the kind of live grenade I would like to throw at the table: "Pro-birth propaganda is nothing but fascist hype." But it would be pretty foolish, as my sister might bear a grudge against me. She's very proud of her children: blond, with turned-up noses, and the terrible twangy voice of little Americans. I wonder how she can manage to be a mother; when it comes to maternal models, we weren't spoiled. Mom was cold, and as austere as Lent. At home, we didn't kiss each other; we didn't touch each other, as though we were separated by a counter window.

Mom looked tough, and her face and hair were pulled back so meanly that she looked like an onion. Mascara, powder, well-cut dresses and window-shopping weren't for her. Having a shopping handicap, she believed that anything that highlighted a woman was vulgar. Hair extensions and French manicure were good for lost girls. Dad, who forever wore an ill-fitting Terylene suit in sinister colors, didn't dress much better. CONSUMPTION IS BAD.

At home, language had to be polished. Every conversation contained a French lesson the way a plum contains a pit. *"What is well thought out is clearly expressed,"* was my mom's favorite saying, followed by the inevitable: *"And the words to express it come easily."*

Today, when I hear people punctuate their sentences with 'like', or to put the word 'just' in front of every adjective, I feel like shouting. It's just, like, stupid.

Mom's linguistic edicts barely concealed her frustrations as a housewife. At the time, people like us didn't have nervous breakdowns, that was just for actresses or people who had embezzled money. Mom was often alone, Dad spent a lot of time in the USSR for his import-export company. "They're tough over there, more so than the Yankees," he used to say with a note of admiration.

Today, my sister works for American capitalists in an investment bank. Her pretentious, slick and superficial husband has a credit card instead of a brain; he's a broker in agricultural commodities, which means he takes our stomachs hostage. Another reason to hate him. He is responsible for the widening gap between junk food and gastronomy ; I shudder when I think of this terrible prophesy: « In the future, only the rich will eat well », says Thierry Marx.

Even if my sister annoys me, what bothers me is looking like a dumbass next to her. I earn twenty times less than she does. I too could have had money, a desirable job and a house at the right address. Besides, there's still time: I understand the secrets of social reproduction really well. I'm related to around ten Who's Who personalities; I'm in the alumni directory of a prestigious university that's at the top of the Shanghai rankings.

The nation's elite? If I want. And it just so happens that I don't. I'm sick and tired of the upper crust, and I'm a refusenik of the bourgeoisie. I'm not punk-rock, I'm punk-rich. The big secret is that the rich are bored. No question of having a life that drags along at a snail's pace. Knowing what the future holds stifles me. Any predefined goal tastes like a consolidated five-year plan. I prefer gambling. Even or odd; pass or fail; yes or no. I publish a book, it sells or doesn't sell; I date a guy, he falls for me or doesn't. Flexicurity is good for Scandinavians dressed in H&M; I'm not flexible and I don't like what's predictable. Fate means betting and playing your luck. I reject ordinary destinies the way you turn away from a tepid dish. I know that one day I'll gamble my life away in a game of Russian roulette, the most elegant way to wrap up the banquet.

Besides, the uncertainty in which I live protects me from any intention of having a child. Children make you fat and that's out of the question. And then I burst out laughing when I hear that our dear little ones are the future: the future is already bankrupt; capitalism is taking over the planet by draining natural resources. So why give birth to Kevins, Dylans, Brandons, Jennifers, Camelia-Jordanas or Cindys? I know what I'm talking about; I too have a commoner's name (sorry, I should say "a popular name.") Admittedly, a first name is used for calling people to the table at dinnertime, but it's also used to know where they come from.

If my name is Corinne, like a beauty consultant in a shopping mall or a tuning enthusiast, it's because Dad wanted a "simple first name" for his daughter. The reason behind the choice was clear: we're not bourgeois.

Or rather, we don't want to be bourgeois. We are close to the people. With a first name like that, it's hard to be a member of the Rotary Club, or to feature in Le Figaro's society columns.

At any rate, thanks for the social stigma, Dad.

I'm sure that if he hadn't controlled his onomastic whims, I would have been named Lenina or Karline. First names that would have subjected me to my classmates' jeers (you don't get more conformist than a kid). But that would be pretty stylish today, as a pen name. *Red*, Karline Zed's new book: neat.

My sister is called Odessa. Yes, like the city. It's an average city in Texas, and Americans have no idea that there's another place by that name, a mythical one, in the Old World. My sister owes her unusual first name to Mom. Unlike Dad, she wasn't Jewish, but she liked Russia, a country she kept inside her like a well-kept secret. Her grandfather had left Crimea a long time ago, and she never missed a chance to remind us that Russia gave France the authors Sasha Guitry, Romain Gary and the Countess of Segur, née Rostopchine.

Odessa, that multilingual and cultured city, was immortalized by Eisenstein's film, *Battleship Potemkin*. A hymn to the revolution and to glorifying the mutiny of the Potemkin sailors in 1905, one of the greatest Communist propaganda films of all times. So Odessa, why not? The billionaire Hilton hotel chain heiress is called Paris - the city of luxury, love and gastronomy, and Kim Kardashian's daughter is named Chicago. Oddly, Baghdad and Damascus are less popular among parents...

As for me, I ended up with Corinne. What was long a handicap now puts me in pole position for a love trip among the lumpenproletariat. Even if I don't know where the word comes from, it reminds me of horrible lumpfish roe, that low-end substitute for caviar. Lumpenproletariat... It's amazing the number of terms referring to the poor. The broke, the beggars, the down-and-outs, the destitute, the poverty-stricken, the needy, the beggars, the starving, the shabby, the proletarians, the penniless, the tramps...

I, Corinne, will wreak havoc among the plebs, the suckers, and the toothless. I'm going to turn heads among those with no air miles (who travel low cost, when they travel.) Those we don't let in, those we seat at the far end of the table. Those for whom eating a Big Mac at McDonald's is a weekend outing. Those who don't have the right family name, who live on the wrong side of the schools map, whose CV always stays at the bottom of the pile, who watch TV programs to which they'll never get invited. Those to whom we reply, "Sorry, that won't be possible," when we give them a reply at all. Those who aren't integrated enough, recommended enough, and who don't have enough connections.

Those who don't know that you don't climb Maslow's pyramid wearing a tracksuit and Nikes. But they can still go to restaurants. In the end, that's the main thing, isn't it? If they have no bread, let them eat cake, as the Queen Marie-Antoinette used to say.

"What are you writing about, right now?" asks Odessa as she arranges pastrami sandwiches on a platter.

"The Russian revolution."

She gives me a disapproving look:

"Don't you think we had enough of that when we were young?"

She has an all-out hatred of Russia, the Revolution, and Communists. Odessa, Version 2 is totally American. Even her French isn't really French. It's become global, it's New York, Paris, London, and Montreal combined.

"I like 1917, voilà."

Edouard barges in, casually:

"Ah, *la nostalgie, camarade...*"

"With your aristocratic name dating back to the Crusades, you wouldn't understand," I tell him. "Since the fall of the Berlin wall, there are more and more wars, more and more acts of speculation, more and more inequalities: in short, more and more shit. No one believes in the post-1989 nonsense any longer: class struggle is over, deregulation is necessary, globalization will benefit everyone, blah blah blah. In short, everything is falling apart. The proof is that I've aged."

The reader will note that I'm more politically cultured. I take the opportunity to blather on about the state of the world. That's the advantage of being left-wing; we have an opinion on everything, which we can share with the whole world. The problem is that we run the risk of being of interest to no one: Edouard absent-mindedly taps on his phone and Odessa yawns.

She snaps back:

"I'm inspired by the future, not the past."

She never dreamed that all men would be brothers, that the poor would be rich, that the rich would be generous, that shepherdesses would become princesses. In her eyes, the revolution is only a short-lived happening. It's not even bankable. My older sister is short-term-oriented. I predict that she'll never go very far in business, because to become massively rich, you have to have historical perspective, a vision.

I'll talk to her using her language, the language of money.

"You know, the past can sell. Just look at *Hamilton's* phenomenal success!"

That musical comedy dedicated to one of the founding fathers of the American constitution is very popular in New York.

She softens up.

"Tell me about it. Impossible to get tickets. The kids would really love to see it."

Edouard sighs and cuts her off:

"Oh no, enough of that show that supposedly symbolizes the American dream...The American dream tires me. I'm hopelessly European."

As he visibly looks at his fingernails, Odessa presents two round, golden cakes on a plate that she places in front of us:

"Now, let's close the history books. Here are some Dominique Ansel *cronuts*! I managed to get some!"

Odessa cuts them each into three pieces, and Edouard enthusiastically shouts out:

"Oh, the *cronut*, that incredible merger of a croissant and a donut...I'm sure you don't have that in Europe. The *viennoiserie* typifies the alliance between France and America! It's the Lafayette of the palate! An ode to the hybrid!"

New York is the mecca of fusion cuisine, that culinary style that blends ingredients and cultures to make a clean break with traditional cuisine. It must be said that in culinary matters, Americans are afraid of nothing. To think that they even invented the term food activist...

Odessa photographs the pastry with her smartphone. She's a great fan of food porn, which consists of taking pictures of one's food and posting them on social networks. To share one's dish breaks down barriers, apparently.

I snicker:

"It's rationed? As in the Soviet Union?"

Edouard replies, with his mouth full:

"Yes. We're only entitled to two *cronuts* per person."

I thought Odessa had only bought two cakes out of stinginess. Or else because she's anorexic, like so many over-qualified bourgeois women. Not even.

Quickly feeling full, as he's perpetually on a diet, Edouard fidgets on his stool:

"Okay, we're going out tonight, girls. We're going to *Forbidden*, there's a Ghetto hype party. Odessa, you should be pleased with yourself for having dumped your little family."

"I miss my children," Odessa objects. "I'm not sure I feel like coming with you."

Sometimes, she takes things so seriously. No wonder I'm the intellectual of the two.

Edouard insists:

"Odessa, you're not actually going to be a couch potato, are you? Watching 'Obesity' on the *Pride* channel, with lots of fat women who've fallen victim to abundance? A total disgrace. You would disappoint me."

Turning to me and winking, he adds:

"You'll see, *Forbidden* is amazing. Full of young people barely past puberty. We're going to set the dance floor on fire."

The stairwell cuts the building's grey monstrosity in half, splitting it open like a huge ripe fruit. I enter the elevator first, where Edouard asks me:

"How are things with the guy you talked about in your text message?"

Odessa interferes:

"Well, well? What's this about? Edouard, since you knew about it, why didn't you tell me anything?"

It's none of her business, but I can't resist the pleasure of shocking her.

"His name is Marco, he's an Italian political activist."

Edouard listens carefully:

"A political activist? Marco... The first name rings a bell... It can't be ...MDG, the terrorist of the '90s?"

He looks at me; I put on a blasé expression. He taps away on his smartphone and, when Marco's Wikipedia page appears, exclaims:

"Corinne, you're taking my breath away here! What a catch... I must say... first-class..."

Odessa looks at me like "I'm reading into your soul." Her voice is a half-tone away from a lecture:

"You want a bad boy from the wrong side of the tracks? And after two weeks, you'll be sick of him?"

What do you expect? I'm more the type to bite into an apple and then put it down. So what? Who does she think she is, lecturing me? A Stalinist secret-police chief?

My turn to drop a Scud missile.

"When you want something, you should never give up on getting it. Isn't that what they say in America?"

"You've always done the opposite of what is expected of you," replies Odessa, shrugging her shoulders. You'll end up in a squat with an empty stomach."

For her, I'm sinking, both socially and financially..

Edouard mediates:

"I found the soundtrack to your love story, Corinne. It's the unplugged version of 'Dynamite' by Taio Cruz."

And he gently hums, like a lullaby:

"Cause we gon' rock this club, We gon' go all night, We gon' light up, Like it's dynamite."

All in concrete and steel, *Forbidden* is located in a post-industrial zone in Brooklyn. Post-industrial: Americans, too, have euphemisms to mean that it's rotten. It's packed with hundreds of wiggling bodies whose energy is overflowing all over the place. Rotating spotlights produce a myriad of colors under the disco ball. The DJ is an inspired despot who sends a goulash of piercing sounds on the dance floor. The three of us bounce around like crazy in a compact crowd of people who could be our children.

Edouard leans over to me and yells in a voice that's loud enough to be heard:

"You know, about MDG...Keep me posted. If you fail... I'll try my luck. Who will win?"

"I dare you."

The next day, I'm sitting in Central Park, near a rock shaped like a giant half-macaroon. This park is totally man-made, designed like a nature reserve in a city that has completely eradicated nature. I'm angry. Some moron has just stopped me from entering the American Communist Party headquarters. Located at 235 23rd Street, it takes up 500 square meters of office space on two floors. Since the 2008 crisis, membership of this microscopic party has increased. Their library is famous, and I was hoping to find documentation on John Reed, an American bourgeois who went to join the revolution in

Russia in 1917. Impossible to get in. At the entrance, an imposing mixed-race guy with a goatee and a ponytail, dressed in a ridiculous batik tunic, tells me I need an invitation. What else? Why not a handwritten note from Khrushchev?

As I discreetly smoke a cigarette to calm down (it's banned in the park, Americans don't mess around with the pleasures of the mouth), a homeless man walks up to me asking for a handout. Really, a poor person here? Why should I give him alms? Charity is a right-wing value. It never changed the world; it only serves to make the rich feel good. Bill Gates created a $40 billion foundation to deflect attention from the fact that his company, Microsoft, has become an expert at the art of tax evasion.

"Hi, my name's Michel."

He speaks English with a strong French accent – the French never lose their accent, even after living abroad for a long time. It makes it easy to spot them from the first word, and to avoid them: depressives and declinologists, they give mournful speeches about the times we live in, like the novels of Michel Houellebecq. They have a hard time pronouncing the words "terrific" or "wonderful." It looks like they've had transfusions of self-hatred and pessimism. To reverse the deadly climate and, above all, to lift their spirits, they exchange addresses of great places to shop for French products: where does one find *cancoillotte* cheese in Vancouver? AAA Andouillette sausages in Goa? A *poularde de Bresse* fattened chicken in Ulaanbaatar?

This pessimist's food obsession is indisputable proof of national decline. Let's at least hope that Paris will always be Paris, the capital of the country that gave us sauces, truffles, Lobster Thermidor, fat geese and *truites au bleu*. A glorious land that has unfortunately failed to instill the fundamentals of gastronomy in the natives it has colonized worldwide.

"I feed myself by going through the trash, I'm homeless..."

There aren't just loaded Frenchies in New York then. What are the civil servants at the French Consulate waiting for to repatriate this Homeless Native? It's really incredible; I wonder what those apparatchiks are being paid for. They must be twiddling their thumbs in their pretty 5th Avenue offices, and with our tax money, to boot. Well, your taxes. I don't have any money, and am non-taxable this year. The tax wars stop with me.

"I have a child to feed..."

Thankfully I have none; feeding myself is enough work as it is. That's not the kind of argument that has the slightest chance of squeezing a coin out of me. Courtesy may be a right-wing value, but I'm very polite with the underclass. *Monsieur, Madame*, please, etc. People of modest means are always stunned, despite their democratic pride, by the affability and thoughtfulness of those of a higher social rank.

"Why don't you start a revolution instead, Monsieur?" I reply.

Dumbfounded, he wonders whether I'm being serious.

I carry on:

"If you've decided to have a child, it's because you hope that one day, his social position will be higher than yours. All parents dream that their children's lives will be better than theirs, but it's an illusion: the social escalator is jammed."

He looks gobsmacked, and keeps quiet. It's time to deliver some recently assimilated concepts. No need to thank me, it's purely out of a spirit of intellectual generosity.

I continue, adopting an educational tone.

"Do you know why? Those who are on the upper floors have intentionally pressed on the 'out of service' button. They're sharing the dough, the friends and the apartments among themselves. They have enough money and connections to get everything and more, to get ahead of everyone on waiting lists. When the billionaire Warren Buffet declares: 'The class struggle is over, the rich have won,' well, he's right. Capitalism is a cannibalistic competition, not the multiplication of bread loaves."

He makes a gesture to leave. Not so fast, I haven't finished. I hold him by the sleeve.

"Monsieur, if you were aware of all of this, you'd refuse to be taken for a ride. You'd spit on the consolation prizes patronizingly passed on to the little people. And you'd go rob the banks, take over the factories, ransack the corporate boards, and burgle the beautiful homes..."

What, he's gone? Unbelievable. So much for breaking my back trying to up the game. These people won't listen.

So, what was I saying? The beautiful homes... Our lovely homes... My train of thought is tangled up like the strings of a Swiss fondue. Our lovely homes... I admit, I consider beautiful homes a birthright. If necessary, I agree to give it up; you can't make an omelet without breaking eggs. Luckily, I learned from an early age to despise ownership through a litany of instructions, which were like commandments: Thou shall not covet plastic junk. Thou shall not clamor for what is advertised in stupid commercials. Thou shall not expect to be offered a miniature tank (a putrid icon of militarism) for Christmas (a consumer-oriented holiday). OWNERSHIP IS BAD.

As I wait for Odessa to get home from work, I settle in the living room. It's comfortable here, more so than Molenbeek. Come to think of it, staying with others is not without charm. That's probably what wwoofing is. I put my computer on a small table in front of the large bay window, with the sky in front of me. By virtue of a few unknown geopolitical agreements, this place has become my place. It's the only place in the apartment where there's a bit of sloppiness, like on an ordinary kitchen table: bills, keys, bowl of overripe fruits, even a book. Hey, Odessa reads? I can't get over it. Better not to look at the title, one of those management books that list all the ways that employers can keep employees on their toes, using corporate jargon. My sister and I live in two parallel realities.

I really want to send a message to Marco, but how can I bypass the Turinese mess? How can I tell him that my supposedly Marxist conference ended in sauerkraut? What about my disappearance from Lingotto? What am I going to come up with? I could tell him that Karl Marx, born in Germany, ate cabbage. Incidentally, how did the great man feed himself? He didn't write about gastronomy, which is a great loss for humanity. Only Friedrich Engels expressed himself, leaving to posterity the strong words: "The proof of the pudding is in the eating." Make of that what you will.

A few days later, I have a date with Edouard on the 54th floor of the Hyatt Time Square.

The rooftop view is splendid. The sun descends into the sea. On the horizon, the light parts into layers, like pasta ingredients that haven't been stirred. The heat lamps and the red woolen robes available for guests protect us from the cold. It's full of beautiful people looking sharp and cool who have come to taste the cocktails of a renowned mixologist.

Edouard asks:

"What's it been like in Europe, since the attacks?"

Dreadful: I'd rather not think about it. The conversation could get heavy. Must avoid the usual words of horrified lamentation: the pathos would ruin the atmosphere.

I reply with a grin:

"Deadly..."

"Ha ha ha. Still, what's happening is appalling."

Quick, must chase away the depressing thoughts. Focus on the present moment, on the impression that one is levitating on top of the world.

"What about you? How have you been otherwise? What's up on the love front?

"Bof, nothing very juicy," he says, shrugging his shoulders.

Edouard orders a New York Sour, a manly mix of scotch and lemon juice, which, according to him, works up an appetite and the chakras. I have a Blow Job, made up of Baileys, Kahlua and Amaretto and topped with whipped cream.

Edouard snarkily remarks:

"The Blow Job, that's very turn-of-the-century."

This snob is of course talking about the 21st century. All the same, he leans over, dips his finger in the cream and gives it a dreamy lick. The libertines' drink, with at least 30 grams of fat. He won't admit it, but it's really good.

"A killer, this thing."

"Better than sex?" he asks, excited by my Turinese adventure.

"Speaking of sex, you know, I think I really like him..."

I want to talk about it, to release something that's coagulating in me in a stifled, compressed way. A bit like vanilla seeds waiting to be released from their pod.

"The terrorist?"

"He's an activist, not a terrorist. He acted to uphold an ideal."

Edouard stares at an invisible point, high up in the sky. He pauses to think.

"You have a point. It was a questionable yet understandable ideal. Not like today's jihadists, these unfuckable, grim-faced, medieval combatants with unpronounceable names. In the end, we miss the old-fashioned terrorists."

"You're a reactionary, I've always known that."

"That's right, what can I say, it was better before," he says with a sigh.

The city shows off its contours against the yellowish-orange sky. That symbol of triumphant capitalism, New York, is a no-go zone for leftists, who forget that it once welcomed millions of misers from Europe. Now gentrified and admittedly a little over the top, like everything that's fashionable, it's popular among French bourgeois, who flee their country in droves. This staunchly anti-nationalist elite leaves the love of France to the little people. Yearning for France is for the poor; the others want the rest of the world.

Bakunin's true children: that's us.

Emptying a ramekin of organic olives, I explain:

"The terrorist and I, it's complicated. I don't know where we stand. Many things take place at the top and not much below."

"If you want to pick him up, let him step forward. Otherwise, he's likely to run away."

"Rather old-school advice..."

"Audacity doesn't pay off in love. Men are afraid of seductresses. That's my personal advice," adds Edouard with an innocent expression.

"And yet...'Only women of great character can make me happy', said Stendhal."

"The ordinary guy is not Stendhal. Being preyed upon freaks him out."

I taunt him:

"A prey! Those little things are fragile."

"You have no idea. Let him simmer and he'll eat out of your hands."

"You know, I hate to wait... I am to romance what Bolino pasta is to cooking: you add boiling water, and bingo, it's ready."

"You're hopeless," he replies. "Sleeping on the first night is like finishing a whole jar of Nutella right after opening it."

"How disgusting, that palm-oil-filled paste that merely serves to get the tongue stuck to the palate and to shut up those who are eating it. It's good for kids..."

"And for the poor," adds Edouard as he finishes his drink. "In

France, they fight to get some. Can you believe it, 500 calories for 100 grams!"

"Is it really over with Hubert?" asks my sister the next day. She's sitting up very straight on the corner sofa of her contemporary, minimalist living room, with its sleek, timeless, and perfectly neutral design. She has disposed of all decorative objects, Chinese pillboxes, candy boxes, plastic flowers, crystal figurines, seashell holiday souvenirs, vases, ducks, gondolas: that's all good for the little people. Her place is a functional, modern space. It's so bare that it's almost...industrial.

"Out with Hubert...I don't know why we divorced, because I don't know why we got married."

"That's too bad. I thought he was really nice."

"Our marriage was reduced to a non-aggression pact defended by START missiles. He thought the women are made to be picked as apples on trees. And he didn't even know how to change a light bulb."

"Don't forget that he introduced you to the people who matter. Do you think that without him, you would have published your books so easily?"

She shuts me up at that point. It's true; it's thanks to my husband that I made a lot of contacts in the French intellectual nomenklatura. The opportunity to publish was handed to me on a silver platter. That's how I avoided the rejections, the countless categorical refusals that are the norm for all beginners in the difficult profession that is writing. But I'd rather cut off my tongue than thank Hubert; I'd rather erase him from my life, just as Trotsky was erased from the Stalinist photos and encyclopedias.

My ex-husband, a prominent journalist, son of a famous historian, nephew of an industrialist, is living proof that, like salad, society needs to be tossed. Forty years old, wrinkled black shirt, messy rebellious-looking hair, an expert in the fresh-out-of-bed look - a fake slob, because in his head he's very straitlaced. It's unlikely that he'd ever commit an incivility, not to mention an antisocial act. He's not the kind of guy you'd turn to for the promise of better tomorrows.

"How about you, Odessa, how's life?"

"Not too bad. When things go wrong, I think of Emmery..."

It's the place where we grew up. A typically French small town located some fifty kilometers away from Paris: the town hall with its geranium pots, the Avenue de la République, the *Café-Tabac*, the post office on the pedestrianized plaza. Odessa goes on.

"And I tell myself that I, at least, left."

I'm happy to hear that my sister sometimes thinks. She's not just a bulldozer. The memory of Emmery bothers me too, like a little strawberry seed stuck in my teeth. Its residents personified the petit bourgeois dream: a house, a car, and two kids. The people of Emmery languished in a closed-minded affluence, in a cautious and dull sense of well-being. There was a lame, all-embracing neutrality that gave off a penetrating smell, like the aroma of a pot of soup that's been simmering for too long.

One of our few distractions was the reading of *Pif Gadget*, a magazine launched by the Communist party.

"Do you remember the spaghetti launcher?"

It was one of the gadgets handed out with Pif. You'd push in spaghetti and pull the trigger; the pasta was ejected "as far as several meters away." Dad was a real stickler on table manners, and we were raised to the tune of "Sit straight," "Don't speak with your mouth full," "Lift your elbow." Also, he didn't find the spaghetti launcher funny. "Don't play with food," he repeated.

I burst out laughing and tell Odessa:

"You see the relationship between Pif and Lenin?"

I don't quite get the relationship between the adventures of the *Placid et Muzo* comic strip and the Communist Manifesto; proof that my left-wing culture is fragile.

Our classmates, with their Lacoste sweaters and their raised collars, subscribed to the ultra-boring *Okapi*, a more conventional read. For them, we were "the Commie's girls," because Dad was a member of the Communist party. A rather cumbersome label that we didn't know what to do with. The left-wing rich man is a walking oxymoron, a bit like a Sumo on a diet. He's hard to classify, and often looked upon as ridiculous.

Wrongly. Because those people, at least, realize that BEING A BOURGEOIS IS BAD. Thomas Piketty, a French economist, is there to make them feel guilty: 80% of global wealth is in the hands of the richest 2%. They have the decency not to complain about paying too much tax, to think of something besides buying Rolex watches and marrying models.

We may not realize it, but being a bourgeois and a leftist at the same time has its advantages. It lets you have it both ways. Heads, the revolution arrives and bingo, something's finally happening, the old world is shaken down to the roots. Tails, the revolution doesn't happen, and it's bingo again: world affairs follow their course, and we sit comfortably expecting glorious tomorrows. In either case, we can pose as a synthetic person, unafraid of historical contractions. It's a win-win situation.

Let's not forget that Marx and Engels were bourgeois, Lenin was a privately wealthy annuitant descended from the lower nobility, and Alexandra Kollontaï, the flamboyant Bolshevik feminist, an aristocrat. As for Giangiacomo Feltrinelli, that extreme-left-wing publisher was the descendant of an extremely rich Italian bourgeois family. A clever businessman, he failed to realize his dream of transforming Sardinia into a Mediterranean Cuba, which I deeply regret: it would have given a boost to that drowsy island and lent an irresistible charm to the unforthcoming Sardinians. The man who handed out leaflets in the working-class suburbs by stepping out of his Cadillac died blowing up an electric pylon with dynamite. (The pylon came out of the blue in this saga. Is it a reference to Lenin's famous sentence: "Communism is electricity plus the Soviets?")

Another picturesque red billionaire, the Frenchman Jean-Baptiste Doumeng, founded a food industry and became a key player in the trade between France and the Soviet Union from 1960 to 1980. During the Cold War, the Communist who had escaped capitalist methods opened an office in Moscow. His private jet safely reached the iron curtain, and he was driven to the Kremlin in a limousine. In other respects, the French Communist Party magnate enjoyed life. Even though he had his napkin ring in the private dining room of Politburo members, he preferred Maxim's and other fine Parisian restaurants to the party headquarters on Paris's Place du Colonel Fabien. That's what you call voting with your fork.

Doumeng had the good idea to die shortly before the world became one country, a right-wing country. There's nothing left of his business. I wonder whether he passed his money to his children, shamefully, obviously shamefully, since inheritance is right-wing. Dad left us nothing in his will. Odessa still has a grudge against him. Not me. Faithful to his principles, he only left behind his ashes, scattered in front of the Wall of the Communards, symbol of the barbarism of the bourgeoisie. (It's a place of remembrance that has three stars in the Left-Wing Green Guide, a book that doesn't exist: I'm prepared to write it.) Of that January day, I only remember the 17 red roses placed on his coffin. Among Communists, death is red.

"Anywhere is better than Emmery," declares Odessa.

She's right. The problem is that I'm afraid Emmery is catching up with me, with its shriveled-up city center, its immediate suburbs, its natural spaces nibbled by semi-detached Phenix homes. Emmery heralded today's world, it was the Russian doll of the suburbs, with pockets of prosperity here and there...and a prison.

Because Emmery had one of France's largest penal institutions. An urban ulcer, a disaster for the town's image. "Oh yeah, I see, Emmery, the prison," people said, making us so damned ashamed in front of the irreproachable kids from western Paris. Still today, my sister and I avoid saying where we were born. When we're asked, we give ourselves the title of Parisian.

Emmery had been split in two in the 1960s by a highway separating the southern residents from the northern residents, the southern residential area from the dense northern housing projects. The latter served as a breeding ground for the people who came to work there, gardeners and cleaning women. As far as I was concerned, for a long time, there were only two social classes: the southerners, people like us, and the northerners, the poor. As for the paternal company's employees, they lived in the south, which proves that they were properly paid. But why do we, the bourgeois, have to keep justifying ourselves?

"Above all, we get Emmery out of our head," declares Odessa.

She and I wanted to leave, to be free, so that those never-ending Sundays that felt as if they lasted a whole month would end. I wanted to live life to the fullest; I wanted to write books, speak ten languages and travel. I planned to go through life like a voracious predator; I wanted to bite into the world as if it were a huge piece of candy, I wanted everything. Cheese AND dessert.

It should also be said that at home, we ate badly. And little. "One must eat to live and not live to eat," was the sad nutritional motto of our parents. It's a well-known fact that gastronomy votes for the right; it's good for the people who exploit the working classes, because they can treat themselves to delicacies. Refinement is not a proletarian attribute. "How does a worker eat? He eats poorly," wrote Mayakovski, a major figure in Soviet literature. So our parents made a point of eating like a poorly fed worker.

I remember pale raviolis, chicken that tasted like fish, slices of rubbery ham, and over-cooked hard-boiled eggs, served sparingly. It's hard for me to forget the meal that was served on my 10th birthday, which consisted of a boiled egg, a canned vegetable medley and (because it was a celebration) petits fours on sale at Aldi. GASTRONOMY IS BAD. It was so Spartan that, today, I indulge in culinary delights with the appetite of the shark in *Jaws*. And as a bonus, the sharp sensation of committing...a Communist sin.

"Shall we have a smoke on the terrace?" asks Odessa. "Can you give me one?"

A transgression for her, given that she obviously doesn't smoke.

"Careful, we mustn't be seen. The whole building is non-smoking," she adds.

"New York is a city full of fascists who stop us from having fun."

For once, I really agree with her.

That reminds me of something. I ask:

"Do you remember Sabrina Varlen?"

Sabrina was our neighbor in Emmery. She was a few years older than me, Odessa's age. She's the one who taught her how to smoke. I know; I watched them through the keyhole. One day, Dad caught them, cigarette in mouth. He was furious, and unleashed the heavy weaponry. Then a Yalta peace agreement was concluded: no more cigarettes within the perimeter of the house. On that subject, do you say within the perimeter, inside the perimeter or in the perimeter? Mom would have had the answer. Too late to ask her. She's buried in Saint-Arnoult-en-Yvelines, not far from Elsa Triolet, nee Iourevna Kagan.

Sabrina's family lived a few minutes away from our stately Empire-style house, whose columns and perfectly straight lines hid inside a big park. The five of them were crammed in a tiny shack overlooking a garage. It was cold in their home, they only heated the kitchen and it smelled of fuel oil; but often there were many people, cousin, friend, neighbour. They were the first plebs that Odessa and I hung out with and, as far as she's concerned, they were also the last. I was aware that we didn't live the same way. Of course, their clothes resembled ours (mail-ordered from La Redoute), and we had the same bikes (bought at the bicycle department of the Carrefour hypermarket at Villiers en Bière.) But their dog was called Johnny; our cat was called Sputnik. They had no idea what the word sport meant when Odessa and I went riding. For them, going on a little trip meant sitting on a folding chair in the forest with an icebox full of beer. Sabrina's parents didn't buy newspapers, and their slim bookshelf was filled with folkloric dolls. They watched TV often, a boon for Odessa and I: TV was banned in our home; it was the glucose-fructose of the eyes. TELEVISION IS BAD.

For some things, the Varlens had good taste. At Sabrina's, we ate well, much better than at our own place. As her father was a cook, he mastered the range of simple, solid, tasty cooking. *Andouillette*, *harengs pomme à l'huile* (herrings with apples), *petit salé aux lentilles* (cured pork belly served with lentils)... My favorite dish was the *tomates farcies* (stuffed tomatoes), with their bright red hats sprinkled with crispy breadcrumbs that melted on the tongue. Their place was a treat for me. I would have stooped to any depths to get invited. In fact, I did stoop pretty low. One day, I claimed that my parents had died and that there was nothing to eat in our house. Even if Sabrina's mother wasn't fooled, she mercifully put a plate in front of me.

Our parents didn't tell us specifically, but they didn't like Sabrina's parents. Was it the difference in social class, or the fact that they were right-wing? A little of both, certainly; to what extent? It would be interesting to find out. Because, yes, our poor neighbors voted badly. Without being ashamed of themselves, without ulterior motives. They were concerned about public safety (who would have thought of robbing their shack?), railed against the abolition of the death penalty (no one ever attacked one of their own), and complained about the number of foreigners (of which there were so few in Emmery.) In 1988, they voted for the far-right candidate Le Pen in the first round of the presidential elections. And for the right-wing leader Jacques Chirac in the second round, maybe because of the French politician's marked taste for calf's head and black pudding.

Their political ideas puzzled me. Dad, as a good *Homo Sovieticus*, explained things as follows: "Sometimes, the masses don't understand, they vote against their class interest, they're alienated by television."

An explanation that was far from satisfactory to me. Why do so many poor people vote for the right? No research fellow, whether from Yale or anywhere else, has provided a convincing explanation for this mystery. Maybe because the poor firmly believe that, one day, they'll get rich – maybe they'll finally be left-wing on that day. And why are so many rich people left-wing? I can explain. Once the rich get tired of the joys of opulence, they undertake a more noble task: to shape a world where money, which is nevertheless their biotope, takes up less space. That's like wanting to make others happy, a sometimes dangerous ambition as no one asked them for anything. In any case, we and the Varlens made up the two sides of those twin-colored school pencils, blue and red. They were blue, we were red. I later understood that a right-wing pleb is no more of a paradox than a left-wing bourgeois.

The Varlens must still live over there. Did they ever dream of leaving? When we left Emmery, we didn't contact them, and didn't hear from them either. To say what, anyway? They say apples and oranges don't mix. A sentence worthy of a concierge, so never to be uttered seriously: that would be tasteless.

Paris, April 2016: the pudding

The Big Apple spat me out, ejected me the way you pop a cork. Or rather, Odessa kicked me out, tired of seeing me be a couch potato in her home. What a bitch, that one, no solidarity. We don't share the same values. What's positive is that I'm getting away from made-in-USA junk food. I'm tired of their ridiculous mimosa cocktails, that acid combination of champagne and orange juice. Tired of their "eclectic" cuisine, cooked in every possible sauce, which seems to be short for "I don't know what I'm doing." I am a patriot of the stomach so I say "vive la France." Besides, this country is the world champion of strikes: proof that there are mysterious connections between gastronomy and protests.

Located in the 16th arrondissement, the apartment where I'm staying allows me to get cozy with Paris while staying down to earth, because it's on the mezzanine floor. This kind of housing is called a *pied-à-terre* among the bourgeois, which means that they don't live there. Aunt Domitille, its owner, also has one in London, for business, and another in Rome, for pleasure. She bought the one in Paris years ago for its very fashionable address, before leaving a France that was, according to her, stifled by administrative inflexibility and confiscatory taxation. A France that was "Europe's last Communist country". If only she was right...It was in New York that she lent me the keys. Admittedly, family is a valuable social safety net when things get rough.

The bad news is that I'll be hanging out with my cousin Gontran, Domitille's son, who's passing through Paris. He's an adopted child; it looks good to adopt when you're bourgeois, it's generous, it's *"I'm rich, but I share."* Odessa and I called him Cherry, because he's the cherry on the cake. He's a young man whose teeth scratch the floor, a completely depoliticized pussy who is finishing his studies in a business school where he's learning the ropes about doing business in a multi-polar world. He's getting ready to start an internship in

Shanghai, as the wealthy don't keep their kids at home long. They have a world to discover, a network to establish. And China is fertile ground: it's where capitalism came out of its wrapping not long ago, like a Kinder Surprise gadget extracted from its chocolate egg.

Before I left New York, Aunt Domitille told me: "It would be great to do some cleaning." The apartment needs it, the carpet is dubious, the bathrooms and kitchen are neglected, the shelves are wobbly: the owners aren't often there. With a simple twist of a rubberized wrist, I turn into Princess Jif, into a madonna of Mr. Clean, with a particularly efficient brand of baking soda. From cleanest to dirtiest, top to bottom, right to left, with south-north/east-west movements. Sweeping. I've come a long way.

Ideally, I should also go to Ikea. What's the point? I wouldn't be able to build their cupboards. Those damn Swedes have democratized manual labor to such an extent that today everyone has to know how to handle a screwdriver and decipher their incomprehensible instructions. Put together their Billy, Lack, Polhem, and chew their Allemansrätten, those disgusting Nordic meatball/mashed potatoes at 6.50 euros a kilo. And to thank progress, capitalism, Scandinavians, anyone you want, but not the cook. We'll see. We'll see with Cherry. I'm overcome with anguish: will he and I have to share meals?

He pushes open the apartment door and says a casual hello. I try to look composed, like those people who think their presence in the world is a given, that the world itself is a given, and that all is in order. Cherry is well aware that I'm the family freeloader, the girl who was born with all the luck in the world, and who takes pleasure in squandering it. His eyes work over me as if I were a clay stain on a piece of greaseproof paper. In his view, I'm about as interesting as an underground miner who's being retrained. There are lots of writers in the family (in France, everyone dreams of being a writer), but they all have another job, a real profession. And those who write full-time have had more success than I have.

Cherry can think whatever he likes, but Stendhal sold very few books in his lifetime, and making a living from writing is nothing but a petit bourgeois fantasy. Art was never profitable, and success seems suspicious to me.

"Hey! You cleaned up! A true white tornado! Did you make something to eat?"

"What else? You think I'm Ducasse?"

At this point in the story, the reader has already figured out that I don't know how to cook. I'm not the type to bring to the kitchen a passion that I bring to nothing else. As your average culinary-deficient person, I will consider working in the kitchen only in the event of extreme necessity (a world war, a tsunami). But that's never happened yet. I opened a can of Chatka royal crab the other day, does that count?

Cherry is unfazed, and opens the fridge. Which is empty, I know. It contains an old piece of Babybel cheese that sags in its plastic wrap. I point out that there's something left in the freezer, a shriveled, dismal slice of pizza.

"Great," he says, and he looks like he believes it, too.

He's ready to conquer the world, unaware that eating has been France's predominant vocation ever since UNESCO ranked French gastronomy as a piece of World Heritage. In the application filed with the international organization to classify the French gastronomic meal, it is stated that it "starts with an aperitif and ends with a digestive, and between the two at least four dishes." What exactly does he learn, in his school for the privileged?

He places the slice of pizza in an oily frying pan, taken out of a cupboard that I haven't yet cleaned. Soon, the smell of rotten food hits me. A faint refectory taste overtakes the room. Nausea starts climbing back up my throat. Hold your breath, think of something else. On the plate, the dough is limp and greasy. I'm on the verge of having a bad trip. It wouldn't take much for me to jump out the window, but the fact that the apartment's on the mezzanine floor makes this gustatory action impossible.

Hunched on a stool, Cherry eats dirtily and much too fast, like a Russian peasant. To interrupt this repulsive vision, I take refuge in my room - which is actually not a room, but more like a storeroom, filled with old pieces of furniture piled on top of each other, an Empire-style rosewood vitrine, an oil painting by a student of Claude Gellée. Aunt Domitille must be reluctant to donate them to the Emmaüs charitable organization. I immediately put my things on a commode framed with maple and engraved boxwood.

These are the relics of an inheritance - unsellable furniture that no one wants anymore. The market for antique furniture has collapsed, overtaken by Ikea's giant blue warehouses. Those who have purchasing power are only interested in 1950s designs: factory lamps, work tables, minimalist chairs, canteen and office furniture. The depreciation of historic furniture is enough to send Auteuil-Neuilly-Passy into despair. Can the penniless people who buy our grandmothers' furniture truly appreciate its solidity, that wood whose patina can only come with time, the resounding beauty and nobility of those objects?

Sitting on my tiny folding bed, I turn on my computer and open up the Red File. I type mindlessly on the keyboard and...suddenly, I manage to write again. The revolution springs from my fingertips, in a silky stream of red and of Cyrillic characters. The words with which to write about it come easily. My writer's block is finally behind me, and my hands fly over the keyboard. A fountain of words pours into the computer. I'm writing the revolution, it's going directly from my veins to the screen. A miracle. (But is there such a thing as a Communist miracle?)

Later, I find a voicemail message from Edouard on my answering machine:

"Did you get back alright from the States? I hope all is well. How is your love story going?"

He adds a link with the explanation: "This is art, useful for navigating on your new Lover's Map." What could it possibly be? He knows I despise contemporary art and its pseudo-subversive poses. All artists think they're rebels, the Che Guevara's of installation art, the Bela Kun's of the camera, when their works merely serve as investments for billionaires. It's a detestable affectation to someone who, like myself, is capable of appreciating real beauty. I was well trained; my parents dragged me to museums from the age of five. Looking back, I think I came close to experiencing the Stendhal Syndrome, that psychosomatic condition that provokes accelerated heartbeat, vertigo, suffocation, and even hallucinations in certain individuals exposed to an overdose of art.

With the education I received, I'm perfectly capable of separating the wheat from the chaff. Nothing moves me more than the asparagus bunch painted by Edouard Manet. A pure masterpiece. It's a small still life in which about 20 pieces of asparagus, tied together with a straw, quietly shimmer. One of my ancestors bought the canvas from the painter in 1880. That same year, Manet made him a second painting: a single asparagus. Even more powerful, even more pared down. It had fallen out of the bunch.

Edouard leads me to the work of Jean-Luc Moulène, a French visual artist who has produced a series of photographs focused on "strike objects." These improbable objects, produced in small batches by workers caught up in labor disputes, are aimed at financing strikes, and don't meet production standards. I click; the photos slide by. Small plastic perfume bottles, kids' shoes, red scarf, spools of wire, printed T-shirts and even dummy bank notes. My favorite object is the "Jobless-opoly", a board game imagined by workers at the Lip watch factory who occupied the factory in 1973. I wonder why the game didn't get mass-marketed, like Monopoly, which was invented by an American job seeker bankrupted by the 1930s economic crisis. The inventors of this game missed a great opportunity to create a start-up, to raise funds and to get rich. Mind you, I'm just saying.

Here, in any event, are pieces of information that are essential to mastering the subject of protests, standing out in demonstrations and being assertive at the barricades. Too bad the history of strike action isn't taught at Sciences Po or at Harvard. It's certainly more interesting than the macroeconomic IS/LM model, or Chomskyan linguistics. And I can just picture myself triumphantly announcing to the charming and straitlaced Aunt Domitille: "Auntie, I passed my Masters 2 degree in Difficult Struggles." She would be shocked; it would be quite amusing. I love my aunt, and you have to be provocative to be kind.

The next day, I'm feeling upbeat, so I decide to make it a left-wing day. Out on the street, I notice clothes abandoned on the sidewalk, near the trash cans. I make sure nobody is looking; if a paparazzi walks by, I'm dead. I can just imagine the headline: "Demise of a great French family: The descendant of an industrial dynasty sifts through the garbage to find something to wear." I look to my right; I look to my left. The jet setters who are thrived on by the press are another branch of the family, but you're never too careful. The street is empty. I quickly grab the clothes. A great way of getting dressed: most of my clothes are back in Molenbeek. I save money I don't have, and spare myself an hour of mind-numbing shopping. I can't understand why so many suckers pile into soulless shops to buy rags produced by Chinese slaves.

They're black items of clothing, well made: a pair of trousers and a long-sleeved sweater. My size, 38. Very wearable, with the subliminal message: *I'm elegant, but don't go thinking this cost me money.* It's the standard *Parisienne* approach: the aim of a piece of clothing is not to make them look beautiful; it's to eliminate status symbols. They're the worthy heirs to Coco Chanel, who popularized a fashion line that's well crafted, yet utterly lacking in affectation - a line that, to the rest of the world, exudes sophisticated indifference. New York women are less hypocritical: when they get dressed, they show off. According to *Vanity Fair*, "They go all the way with their beauty." My black clothes will help me look good for work appointments. Looking like a starving woman is not good for business (nor is looking like a millionaire, but that's not about to happen to me).

Then I go drink a Picon beer at the *Rendez-vous du Périf*, a little café at the Porte de Clignancourt. When you live in a fancy area, it's important to get close to real people (real people: a right-wing term used to refer to lower-class France). I leaf through the *Parisien* newspaper on the counter, and I read my horoscope. It's encouraging: *Something will happen in your love life. Be ready.* I scratch a Morpion scratch card after a moment of perplexity: should the card be scratched with one's nail, or with a coin?

It's actually super-easy to be left-wing.

When you're successful at something, you immediately need to take on a new challenge by raising the bar. To always surpass yourself. So I take a notebook out of my bag and try writing in the manner of Annie Ernaux. This novelist advocates a left-wing style of fiction writing: flat, cold as a knife. Here's what I write, in a very *Ernautian* style: "This is not a biography - nor is it a novel, naturally. My father, who was born in a domineering milieu, had to become ancient history for me to feel less lonely and less of a fraud in the world of words, where, without his ever wanting it, I ended up."

On second thought, I'm not sure about adopting a left-wing writing style.

Reader, are you still there? To wrap up this day with a strong gesture, I decide to call you "comrade reader." What do you think?

In Paris, nostalgic publishers like to meet authors on the Left Bank - ever since, for cost-saving reasons, most publishing houses moved to working-class areas. A relocation that came as a veritable blow to the Parisian intelligentsia, because it was at its best when it was concentrated in a tiny area situated between Saint-Germain-des-Prés and Odéon.

There are two categories of publishers, the young and the old. They're a bit like cheese. The young ones still haven't picked up the mannerisms of the Parisian cultural bourgeoisie. It takes just a decade for the young publisher to turn into a pitiless arbiter of stylistic and narrative elegance, into the self-proclaimed guardian of the temple of the French language. Soon, he or she will be the one who knows, who demands, who decides, and who ends up believing that his or her contribution to the book, generally minimal, is absolutely crucial. Nothing pleases a publisher more than to have an author tickle their ego by referring to "our book," "our project." By the time the publisher reaches the end of his career, he or she will be using the royal "we" when speaking in the first person.

I have an appointment with the publisher who published my Stendhal a few years ago. I have to sell him a project : that's why I am in Paris. Highly pretentious, he belongs to the second category: that of cured cheese. Jacques doesn't understand much about politics. Thankfully, he's left-wing, and here's the proof: he wears corduroy trousers and a baggy jacket, and his hair is thick and fuzzy like cotton candy. My interlocutor necessarily views himself as a resistant, like the hordes of literary people who all went underground. All of these cigar-smoking insurgents, these armchair revolutionaries, don't deserve the impending insurrection.

If Paris is well worth a mass, October is well worth a salad. I throw in the hypocritical words: "How I would love to work with you. Your new imprint, *Full stop*, is superb." While I've never once opened any of the books in the imprint, I can well imagine their detached/implied, objective/subjective, politically incorrect/salutary orientation. It pulls together books by members of the French intellectual landscape, their friends and their children - full stop.

Others can go get read somewhere else. The imprint provides an excellent excuse not to publish them. Respecting its coherence, its editorial line, allows the publishing house to keep away the villains who pretend to be writers, the nobodies who come out of nowhere, wet behind the ears, with a manuscript under their arm. Well, yes, what would happen if everybody started writing? The publishing world is drowning in manuscripts. Too many texts, too many books. The quantity goes up, the quality comes down, and we're verging on the low cost. Don't people have anything better to do? For example... work?

"I have a great project for you, Jacques."

"Interesting. It's, um, about the Russian revolution, right?"

I plunge right in - it's make-or-break time.

"Yes, it's 100 years old, can you imagine? 1917-2017: there's an editorial opportunity not to be missed."

"Can you give me a quick summary?"

"In 1917, Russia is a backward country, and ..."

"Sorry to interrupt, I forgot to ask: would you like to eat something?"

"With pleasure."

He invites me to have lunch with him on expenses, meaning paid for by his publishing house. A good idea, given the state of my bank account, even if I'm somewhat wary of these constrained and very coded moments where you have to be careful not to splutter or get a stain.

Here's a little instruction manual for the work lunch, that pillar of French savoir-vivre. The common practice is to order just one dish, because you have to show that you're there to work, not to scarf down a succession of dishes behind your tie. The 'neither-nor' is therefore de rigueur: neither too economical (that would suggest low self-esteem), nor too expensive (that would suggest demands that are incompatible with the limited budgets of the book world). It's also recommended to eat neither too fast (glutton) nor too slowly (slug). To be neither too dirty (it would be impolite) nor too clean (you'd seem fussy). A slightly casual attitude is acceptable, if not recommended, to show your opposite number that you're comfortable playing the social game. And you need to watch your gestures: don't run your fingers through your hair, don't adjust your bra straps, don't play with your necklace or pull up your tights. *Bon appétit* all the same - even if wishing each other "Bon appétit" is in bad taste because it's a reminder that you're also a belly.

"The *plat du jour* is tempting," he says, thinking hard about it.

The ABC's of psychology demand that you choose the same thing as the person you're courting.

"Why not? So, as I was saying, the Soviets embrace the ideas of the Bolsheviks, and the provisional government, powerless and discredited..." At that moment, Jacques's smartphone starts vibrating. He gets up and excuses himself.

When he sits back down, the dish is served.

"Oh, nice, their *choucroute* (sauerkraut). I like it when it's cooked this way. Or with fish - have you ever tried that?"

"No, I prefer *choucroute* cooked the traditional way..."

Oops, I took my eye off the ball. The gastro-worshipping publisher, busy chewing on a sausage, led me off track. In fact, he trapped me without even realizing it. I have to regain control of the situation. It's going to be hard, because he adds:

"Look, at the next table they ordered *le vol-au-vent*... It's the first time I've come here since they changed owners. Sorry, I interrupted you."

"At the head of the Petrograd Soviet, a revolutionary military committee takes control of the strategic locations in the city. The insurrection is launched on October 25..."

His smartphone vibrates again. I feel like I've lost the match, there's no sense in carrying on. Regrettably, I spare him the armed uprising, the dissolution of the provisional government. I skip over the decrees that give land to the peasants, establish worker controls over production, and end the war with Germany. With a heavy heart, I drop the strong measures that establish gender equality, divorce and abortion. Farewell to Lenin and his goatee, which floats in the wind.

With heavy eyelids, Jacques mutters:

"You know, I have to tell you, I don't believe in the Russian revolution. The subject matter doesn't allow conceptual asides, or strong re-problematizations."

We've touched the core of the issue, formulated in Parisian intellectual jargon: he's not interested. To his credit, Jacques says it like it is, which has become a rare thing. No one ever says no. "We're thinking about it, we'll get back to you very soon" is the usual blah-blah used to leave everything hanging, especially your interlocutor. Never commit, never back out: the neither-yes-nor-no is the leitmotif of our times. In France, we're particularly good at the diplomatic mysteries of the non-answer.

"While we're at it, what if you wrote something more (he says, coughing slightly) commercial?"

I don't reply. Who does he think I am? I will not give in to the siren songs of easy success and flashy notoriety. It would be a worse betrayal than that of Ramon Mercader, who passed himself off as a journalist to approach Trotsky and assassinated him with an ice pick.

Noticing my staggered expression, he tones things down:

"If you're really committed to the revolution, it could work as a historical novel. Something light, easy to read, with a love story. It wouldn't be for *Point à la ligne*, of course, because we pay great attention to style. You see, there has to be a style, a true critical sensibility."

When this paragon of fine writing pronounces the word "style," his nostril trembles. Is it because I'm a woman that he speaks to me in this slightly condescending tone?

I take a deep breath. Emotional neutrality. Zero harshness. Everything's under control. He won't know that I'm capable of biting. I order a little *mirabelle* plum brandy to take it all in. I down it in one. I calm down. As the Italian proverb goes, *Non cessar per gli ucelli, di seminar i piselli* ("Don't give up seeding on account of the pigeons.")

I leave the brasserie talking to myself. You're never better listened to than by yourself. So as I was saying, on October 25, 1917, having taken control of the bridges, the stations, the telephone networks, the Bolsheviks charge on the former Imperial Palace. It falls like a ripe fruit. The insurgents then rush into the cellars to drink the fine vintage wines that are kept there. A giant fiesta begins. In the Romanovs' very abundant cellar, the drinking session lasts several days. In a Dionysian moment, the crowds drink Château d'Yquem.

At that point in my self-narration, I stop smack in the middle of an avenue, amidst a cacophony of honking horns. What happens next? The revolutionaries, determined to restore order, give instructions for the wine to be poured out on the street. Horror: bottles of Romanée-Conti, of Petrus, of Chambertin, poured into the gutter! A revolting act of barbarity.

Passersby give me a very strange look. I'm worried that the men in white will come and take me. (Is it Professor T who sent them to me?)

I walk a long time to overcome my paranoia. Year after year, Paris's Left Bank, once a Bohemian area, looks cleaner and cleaner, with its brick facades and impeccable sidewalks. The renovated boulevards, the health and nature outlets, the nutrition and balance ateliers, the Ayurvedic massage places and the child spas flourish on what's starting to look like a country club. I look at the ads in a real-estate agents' window. Question: how many books would I have to sell to live in the area? This high-flying mental calculation would take far too much time. Such mind-numbing speculations are good for my accountant. Let's say too many, way too many books.

When Paris still had populous areas (populous: the pejorative version of popular), Lenin lived near the Parc Montsouris. I make a pilgrimage to the 14th. arrondissement, to 4 rue Marie-Rose. It has to be the soppiest street name in Paris, so ill suited to the Lenin Museum which was once located there. Closed in 2007, it was situated in the apartment where the exiled Vladimir Ulyanov stayed from 1909 to 1912. He led a quiet petit-bourgeois life there, surrounded by women who were all devoted to the great man: his wife, his sister, his mother-in-law and his mistress. A veritable harem. I notice with a heavy heart that even the plaque has been removed.

I go back home and lie down on my bed, feeling discouraged. Jacques sure has nerve, a historical novel...? A real-fake love story between Lenin and Empress Sissy, for example? Ridiculous. When Lenin's real life is itself a novel. As told by Dad, it took on epic dimensions. Once upon a time, there was a young man named Vladimir who led a carefree life in the comfortable family estate of Simbirsk, on the banks of the Volga. One day, tragedy strikes. His older brother is sentenced to death for having taken part in a plot to assassinate Alexander III. He is subsequently hanged.

Act two. In 1917, Vladimir Ilyich Ulyanov, also known as Lenin, by now a professional revolutionary, comes back to Russia. He travels on a mysterious sealed train car to Petrograd, and the icy hand of vengeance travels with him. The train allows Lenin and his entourage to leave Switzerland and travel across Germany unencumbered, right in the middle of a war. Because it's the Germans who allow him to return home after 17 years of exile: the aim is to spread the plague among their Russian enemies by catapulting a notorious troublemaker into the country. As they predicted, Lenin overthrows the hated Czarist regime, which weakens the Russian bear vis a vis its neighbor. And the boomerang is back where it started when, in 1918, a Communist revolution inspired by the Bolshevik October takes place in Germany. That's how Lenin avenges his brother by spreading his ideas: from east to west, from right to left, and from top to bottom. The right way. Merciless.

The reader, even the left-wing reader, will find this paragraph too long, but it's important to educate the people. Even in a commercial book. Especially in a commercial book.

All is not lost on the book front. Every time a door closes, another one opens. A contact's contact's contact gave me the details of a young, bold and sharp publisher whose surname is famous among the French intelligentsia. Things move along fairly easily, because she has heard of me. My last book sold 30,000 copies. Once upon a time, that would have been "a good sale," but nothing special. Nowadays, it's a bestseller. In her eyes, I'm a golden goose.

A few days later, I meet Audrey. She finds Saint-Germain-des-Prés completely passé and prefers to have work meetings in trendy areas. It's 10 a.m. in a super-cozy café in the 13th arrondissement, much too early to have any hopes of getting invited to lunch.

Audrey is dressed casually, in scruffy boots, slim jeans and a raincoat with a brand I won't mention. Her outfit conveys the intended message: *Please don't take me for a banker, a trader or a lawyer.* She is nicer than Jacques, more down-to-earth. Aware of economic realities, she knows she's in the hot seat. Soon her job will be outsourced, and she'll be a contract worker, like her authors. Welcome to the club of the culturally doomed.

To get the conversation going with a bit of small talk, I ask:

"How's the book market?"

"Oh la la...Too many books, not enough readers..."

It's the usual complaint you hear from French publishers, who don't think to blame themselves and ask if the little apolitical novels that they publish truly interest the public. Novels that never speak of the economic conditions of book production, as if it were some chef's secret that the reader should never find out about. Women come from Venus, men from Mars, and books from the sky.

"The less people read, the more they write," she goes on. "I receive more manuscripts than I sell books."

I imagine Audrey drily telling one of her young authors as they sign their first book deal: "We're not here to talk money, we're here to talk books."

It's the moment for me to make a clever transition to the subject that interests me:

"Do you know that in the Communist world, everyone read books?"

"The Russian revolution... It was Marx who took power, right? Or was it Lenin?"

Not surprising, in a profession where lack of education proliferates like wild weed. It's always the cobbler's children who go barefoot, cooks, who eat the worst food, doctors who get the worst treatment (although Professor T., who's ubiquitous on TV, looks fit as a fiddle). I'm going to fix that. I take the pleasure of briefing her on the Russian revolution. The fall of the Romanov dynasty, the assault on the Winter Palace, the manly workers, the robust realism that speaks directly to the soul: I give her a little history lesson while drinking a coffee. I barely look at the waiter (no one ever looks at the waiters, the bouncers, the delivery guys).

Audrey opens her mouth and says "It's very interesting, but..." which doesn't bode well.

"The problem," she says, "is that some left-wing repenters, very influential, waged a deadly war on the revolution that they had so dearly loved. Even today's left are wary of them: they prefer the Spanish Republicans, for example. Which reminds me, you could write something about them," she suggests.

Discouraged, I put all my intellectual capacities into this sentence, borrowed from Jacques: "I don't know if this allows conceptual asides, or strong re-problematizations..."

Truth be told, the losers of history, those who failed to start a revolution, are not my cup of tea. I prefer winners.

As Audrey asks for the bill, I realize that the waiter is super-sexy. Exactly my kind of guy, I who love dark blue-eyed guys like Daniel Craig, the actor who plays James Bond. Unfortunately for his female fans, agent 007 is a hardheaded anti-Communist.

"I have to think about all of this. We'll be in touch," she says as she walks out. "I'll keep you posted."

I don't know where I stand. Is it yes or is it no? The publisher, who masters the art of not taking sides, would have fit right in at the Bandung Conference of Non-Aligned Nations.

The waiter comes and goes between the tables, and his jeans, which he wears low on the hips, reveal the white band of his underwear. His T-shirt clings to his biceps and his torso. He swings often, more and more often, around the table where I'm sitting.

Mechanically, I break up into little crumbs the speculoos cookie that comes with the coffee. This Belgian cookie has spread like wildfire in Europe - unfortunately in an industrial form (absence of spice, too-soft brown sugar) that's an insult to the original. Neapolitan pizza and paella met a similar fate, proof that to conquer is to betray.

I now observe the waiter's comings and goings. He sends me eager little looks, as if I was the prize in a jackpot or a Christmas dinner. I feel irresistible. Talking about revolution has made me look beautiful. It's brought wind to my sails, color to my cheeks and a twinkle to my eyes. Suddenly, he lunges at me and hands over his business card.

"My name is Benji. I live in Paris. I'd like to buy you a drink one of these days."

Benji... Would that be an abbreviation of Benjamin? Or is it a dog's name? He has a cheeky humor. He has a thick Parisian accent.

The voice is a ruthless social giveaway, even more so than the look. It's the kind of vocal nuance that I immediately hear, because I obviously speak the language of the upper classes, the one that is said to be unaccented. In truth, it's the French spoken in Paris, in an articulated and light form, without the guttural tone that comes from the back of the throat. Years ago, my speech was standardized by fanatical teachers determined to get rid of regional accents and words coming from the suburb.

"I'm Coco. Coco as in Corinne, not as in Colombe."

Colombe is my cousin, a *bourgeoise*. I mean a real *bourgeoise*, not one who betrays the best interests of her social class, like I do.

He's really cute – more metrosexual than bad boy, but I can live with that.

Back at Cherry's, I google Benji's name. And...by Trotsky's spectacles! I find out that the guy I took to be a waiter leads a café managers' union, an organization that's none other than a right-wing lobby. He's not oppressed; it's a case of mistaken identity. Benji fights for the right to fire people, opposes the government's fiscal racketeering. An appalling right-wing stance. At the same time, he's attractive...what to do? Contact him anyway? A superficial fling would be welcome; I'm starting to get tired of the cross-border flirt that I'm caught up in.

Finally, in the name of coherence between the superstructure and the praxis, I give up on the hookup with Benji. It's hard for me, but I'd rather not eat food of that sort. When you're left-wing, you can't sleep around. I'll sleep alone: being left-wing is like converting to a religion. I deserve the Hammer and Sickle medal, and I award it to myself.

To be admirable without being admired is uninteresting, and I write to Edouard to tell him about it.

"I met a gorgeous guy. Unfortunately, he's right-wing. I've given up. Do you think I did the right thing?"

No reply to my message. It shows that he doesn't understand the interesting moral dilemma that I'm facing. I know him; he'd be capable of doing deals with the devil and sleeping with a handsome Nazi so long as he finds the guy attractive. Edouard is truly *pre-fascist*; the permafrost of Norilsk or Kolyma would set him straight. To top it off, he'll tell Odessa everything. And she's going to turn it into a joke for her right-wing friends (a tautology). What gossips, those two. But since everybody is talking about it, then it's official: I'm left-wing.

Now, I have every right to visit the Lenin Café. It's Europe's last Lenin Museum, located in Chalonnes, in Maine-et-Loire. Given how enriching contact with the France of below is, I initially thought about going there by car-pooling. But the train is more Russian: the exoticism of the Trans-Siberian railway, Anna Karenina throwing herself under a locomotive... The Soviets topped it off by building a gigantic railway to link the cities on a territory nine times bigger than today's European Union. Overtaken by their passion for the railway, they created a Ciné-train for propaganda use. One of its engines, dubbed October Revolution, went up and down the country to spread the message of the revolution through a mix of poetry, posters and films.

Arriving in Angers with the train, I jump out of the train car to escape the unbearable promiscuity of screaming kids. Like Lenin, who had no children, I don't see why I'd like kids, why I should go all nice and coochy coo with them. In fact, I don't know why I'd be nice at all. Nice people don't change the world, they don't make history. I can be unpleasant in three languages (let's say three-and-a-half including German), and that's not within everybody's reach. Kindness, that sugary business of our times, is no more than a smokescreen skillfully used to conceal the violence of class interactions.

I get on a bike. It's a Leninist mode of transportation, since Lenin rode a bicycle, but some leftists don't know that; it's time to set the record straight (there, done). Bags weighed down with a piece of fried-pig bread and a prune pâté, I'm all set for adventure. It's springtime, and the sun maliciously toys with the tree leaves. The surface of the Loire River has the deep and smooth sweetness of liqueur. The wind gently slices through the air, a fragrant wind that feels like it could be licked like an ice cream cone. There are vineyards everywhere. Ah, Loire Valley wines, what a treat... The words Layon and Savennières make my mouth water like a Pavlovian dog.

Off I go, riding my bike along the Loire, on an 800-kilometer cycling path that's unique in Europe. On my back, I'm carrying Cherry's "two-second" tent, a leftover from boy scout Sundays. He doesn't use it anymore, and I didn't even have to confiscate it in the name of the revolution. "Very easy to set up," he told me earlier, adding, with a touch of commiseration: "Even somebody like you can set it up. It's as easy as pie." Easy as pie means: watch out, there are logistical problems ahead.

I pedal away, surrounded by social democrats enamored with the Scandinavian model who are here as tourists. They represent a peaceful strand of humanity, practicing a sweet and calm form of coexistence. They've rooted evil and war out of history the way you would pull a bad tooth out of a gum. I pursue a committed and militant objective, which allows me to look down on them.

The aim now is to find the Lenin Café, and it's no easy task. The Loire is a giant river, as vast as the Volga. It's impossible to find one's way in this tangle of islands, of bends and arms. I get lost and lost again. I cross one bridge then another. Where am I? I'm sure Lenin never came here. He was doubtless wary of these lost corners. Was there ever a revolution in Cucugnan or in Saint-Leu-sur-Tremoing?

Night is beginning to fall. The sides of the road look chewed up. I finally arrive on the island of Chalonnes. According to the map, it has the shape of a long and thin string bean. The place is flat and sandy, with an end-of-the-earth look about it.

Finally, I find the café: it's the place where there are lots of people. The Lenin Café is celebrating its 10th anniversary. At first, you visit the cabin-like museum, with its low-ceiling rooms. Martine, the founder of the place, is a Communist who specializes in Eastern European public finances. She's brought together all the kitsch Soviet bric a brac that nobody wants anymore. Plaster busts of Vladimir Ilyich, posters, flags, Komsomol scarves, etc. And books, of course. The library reminds me of my parents' library. You look at the books in a state of contemplation. The tables feel like they could start turning any minute. Lenin, are you there? You don't dare touch anything. Yes, Madame, there are thefts; we have to be careful. A medallion representing baby Lenin has disappeared. One day, it'll be worth a fortune at Christie's or Sotheby's.

Outside, a Russian orchestra with sobbing balalaikas is busy playing. People have borscht and sit casually at big tables. The locals join in, as do leftists and even (yes, yes) rightists. There's a kind of class bonding. Martine is a magician. You drink. Not vodka but wine. Oh, the fabulous verticality of these local wines, structured like a Moscow subway station.

Ah, the Savennières, with its power, its strength and its poise, compensated by that mineral taste...It's quite simple: this wine is not the baby Jesus in his velvet trousers, it's young Lenin in his fur chapka.

Tchin-tchin! Along the Loire, you pronounce it more informally as "chin-chin." This expression used for clinking glasses was originally a reference to China, "Chine-chine." Now there's a word that all languages adopted: clinking glasses is a mark of trust. When you clink glasses, you don't kill each other. I toss my glass over my shoulder as the Chinese lanterns are turned off.

There's a payback time for everything. Numb with cold, I wake up early in the morning in a field, under the quizzical eye of a roaming donkey. It's as if I had spent the night crossing a forest in the Urals, between a pack of wolves and fugitives from the Siberian mines. I obviously never managed to set up Cherry's tent, which turned into a messy knot with the repeated assaults of my clumsy hands. A rip-off, this scout's tent. Not surprising: the father of the scout movement, Baden Powell, was a fascist.

I painstakingly manage to get on my bike saddle and pedal to the closest café. A cup of hot coffee and a croissant save me from hypothermia. What a delight to dip the croissant in the cup. The moment when the jet-black liquid covers the white pastry is uniquely sensual. I let the horn of the croissant soften. The bitter beverage permeates the pastry and seeps through its generous and rich layers. A rush of joy overtakes me as I indulge in this illicit pleasure, which was forbidden when I was a child on account of hygiene and good manners. It's divine, I even allow myself to lick my lips. A total breach of etiquette!

At the counter, Parisians talk to the café manager. I immediately have them figured out by the way they talk: bourgeois with advanced university degrees that dream of living in a peaceful place far from the stress of traffic jams. They own a vegetable patch. Mankind has turned into a hobby the activity that once brought it wealth and civilization: the slave has become the master. It won't be enough to feed them. They plan to open a tapas bar to reconnect with the concept of work. Right now, food-related professions are all the rage. Hotel and restaurant management schools, which used to be reserved for dunces, are submerged with applications. Studying law smells of mothballs, business schools are not what they used to be, and a vocational certificate in cooking is much more hip. Working for the Rothschilds? Don't even mention it - you shall be a cook, my son.

At first sight, Chalonnes-sur-Loire (population: 6000) has nothing going for it. A banal little town, debonair and nonchalant, where there seem to be no rich people and no poor people. Where are they? The Gini coefficient, that measure of inequality, is probably verging on zero - in other words, on perfect equality. Class struggle? No sign of it. All things considered, the social democrat's paradise has attractive assets that are not to be overlooked. Besides, rental rates are so low that if I lived here, I could afford a Cleanliness Expert. A cleaner, if the comrade reader prefers. A cleaning lady + an egalitarian way of life: it's called having your cake and eating it too.

Going back to Paris is hard. I haven't checked my voicemail messages for a few days, which makes the wait 10 times longer. No news of Marco. His silence is a blatant violation of the Geneva conventions: emotional bribery, sleep deprivation, I should drag my executioner to court. My body is giving way, there's an acidity discharge from my esophagus, that organ that I can't manage to locate is certainly burning and viscous. I feel like a jacket potato, all dried up in my aluminum outfit.

Unable to stand it any longer, I write to him and put my foot in it.

"Marco, I love you. I cannot forget the glorious light that came into my life on that winter's day in Turin. When can I see you? It's enough for me to close my eyes to feel your presence, the taste of wine on your lips, your mouth pressed over mine. I would like to relive every instant of the minutes spent on that terrace, to caress them and keep them gently close to me, like frail and precious dreams."

It's what's called a major offensive strategy. In a flash of clairvoyance, I realize that it's a serious mistake. MDG will think I've gone off the rails, that I'm a love addict poaching on the blue lawns of passion. And unfortunately, he will be right.

From a strictly stylistic standpoint, my letter is pretty well written. My little secret: it's plagiarism. I copied a letter written by the Communist photographer Tina Modotti. Theft? No, a simple passing of the baton from one comrade to another, since Tina worked for the Kremlin. That letter was destined for one of her lovers. Since no one writes love letters anymore, I was at a loss for linguistic elements. Thanks to Tina, I have the recipe: 100 grams of feeling, 20 milligrams of emotion, and a pinch of oenology... And you stir until you get an emulsion.

No reply. I go around in circles and turn into a languid, empty-eyed Barbie doll, a prisoner of my screen like an egg in aspic. It's a question of survival; I must absolutely get away from my computer. Go back home to Molenbeek? It would be worse. Staying alone in my one-bedroom apartment and getting depressed at the sight of a brick wall is not a solution.

Why not go into training to get her mind off it? Writers rarely train, unlike the rest of the population, which spends its life getting trained to learn new skills that disappear one after the other. And yet picking up new skills is exactly what writers need to open up to the world, because they have a tendency to be narcissistic and to write... French novels. Self-fiction, with a lot of self and not a lot of fiction.

Professional training is a right, and I want my share. Not so long ago, among Communists, there were red circles, study groups, management schools where militants could be educated. They served to transmit the culture of the dominated and to give them the intellectual tools to tackle fascinating questions, such as: "Have productive forces stopped growing?"

Little is left of that education, despite its effectiveness. That's where Europe's most powerful statesmen, Vladimir Putin - ex-KGB agent - and Angela Merkel learned everything. The German Chancellor was educated in East Germany, where she got her Ph.D. (admittedly in natural sciences, a field that's considered ideologically neutral) before becoming a researcher at the Academy of Sciences. As part of her studies, she wrote a text entitled "What is the socialist lifestyle?" Good question, what is the socialist lifestyle?

I would really like to know. Angela's dissertation could offer clues if only I spoke better German. Too bad, my first foreign language was Russian. For my parents, it was the language of the Communists - and for the other students' parents, a scholastic strategy to be "part of the right class." That's how, by a ruse of history, I did all of my studies with bourgeois students. And that's how I never got a chance to meet bad students, those who spoke in slang and wore high-top Jordans. Those who smoked joints, who tinkered with scooters and who plotted trouble in the quiet nights of Emmery. The bad boys I so wanted to go out with.

Today, Russian is the language of oligarchs and of Eastern European whores. I don't get a chance to speak it often. I gave up Russian, but not mixing with rebels. To get close to them, I found a workshop that was open to militants from the entire left-wing galaxy, Communists, ecologists, mutineers... The aim is to work on your speech abilities, what's called storytelling, a word that's banned on the left. No need for connections or hotlines, you just have to pay, and it's not expensive. I borrowed money from Odessa, because I find pleasure in the idea that she should be filling the coffers of a left-wing organization. If she knew, she would make a big song and dance out of it.

It all starts at the Gare du Nord. That multimodal hub is organized like a *mille-feuille*: the upper layer is reserved for the rich, with the Eurostar that goes to London, and the lower layer for the poor, the pale *banlieusards* who take the regional express network between Paris and the suburb. They overlap and ignore each other. I reluctantly head for the bowels of the city, because the regional network is *terra incognita* for true Parisians. And right now I'm a dyed-in-the-wool Parisian, as Parisian as the actresses in Sex and the City are New Yorkers.

I get lost in a sticky labyrinth of hallways painted in uncertain shades. Here, there's no sense of chromatic harmony: no need to look very far to encounter an epidemic of vandalism and a flare-up of incivility. Dressed in such a way as to melt into the crowds, in a grey sweater and jeans, I'm in tune and completely invisible.

As a result, the person who comes to pick me up at Villiers-en-Brel station has a hard time finding me. Two of my future classmates arrived on the same train. We end up finding and meeting each other. They're seasoned militants who are active in several associations whose names I try to remember. One is a true Stakhanov of protests: she juggles with acronyms, with first names and with demos. Her coded discourse is only aimed at insiders. She reminds me of Tante Diane, a patroness involved in a number of charity organizations. It's not just the poor who want to pay in kind.

The trainees are housed in a prefabricated building that usually hosts corporate seminars. I left my wheelie suitcase in Paris, because it's much too evocative of the globalized middle class.

I put my backpack on the floor in a room where another trainee has already settled in. She's thrown her jacket on the only available chair. Her ultra-tight clothes highlight a lazy weight problem, the one that affects poor people, because the others are sent by their parents to an endocrinologist who recommends that they eat lots of fruit and cut back on carbohydrates. She's a caricature of the girl from an underprivileged background - I'm talking about the poor of today, not the little white proletarians like the Varlen, our old neighbors, who already look so 21st-century old-fashioned.

She and I look at each other. Everything divides us. The obese North African girl from the suburb / the skinny, preppy blonde: it's war.

"Hi, I'm Samia, I come from the nine-three."

The nine-three, in other words the Seine-Saint-Denis, is a real poor people's ghetto. Clearly, I chose the right internship.

"Hi, I'm Corinne. I'm from the seven-seven. More specifically, from Emmery."

She bounces right back.

"Oh yeah? The prison?"

She smiles. I cleverly pulled out a popular reference. It's surprising for a prison to open doors.

"Almost!"

People who haven't passed their A-level are, to me, ethnological curiosities worth studying. Here's an idea: what if I did an undercover reportage about them? It could be grounds for a humanist story about the real life of ordinary people, the "real people." The sort of books the cultural bourgeoisie love to write on the "voiceless," the very people it does everything to silence and make invisible by standing in their way absolutely everywhere. With a bonus "wet T-shirt" evening, like on campsites, places where I've never set foot? I'm sure that in the collective showers, things happen that preppies could never imagine.

Samia is more interesting than the other trainees. They belong to the middle class, the kind that is quickly proletarianizing and that wants to get into the ring to fight back. There's an unemployed person, a female electrical engineer who is growing saffron, a guy who was made redundant by Société Générale, a militant ecologist and a specialist in bio-mimicry (?). I'm disappointed. Where are the real proletarians, those fierce and determined soldiers? The workers with the callous hands, the valiant working women? Where have all the toiling masses gone?

The Internet site of the newspaper *L'Humanité* should help us track them down. If there are six million proletarians in France, they're invisible, below the radar. Swallowed by the soft underbelly of the middle class, a middle class that's more and more... popular. It's not the Internet site of *L'Huma* that's going to politicize them; French Communists have consigned the hammer and sickle to the attic. That's why their electorate is so weak. No pain, no gain.

The workshop begins. We're sitting on chairs with tablet arms, like in corporate seminars; usually, business plans are drawn up in this place. Outside, two ailing pines wilt beneath the grey skies. Two militants run the daylong workshop: François and Frédéric. Surnames are banned. They both handle smartphones, even though these gadgets are not very popular in Leftie-land.

I flaunt my year-2001 cellphone, meaning dating back to telecoms prehistory. I'm proud of it; it's a collector's item. They don't understand that I'm showing off. To them, this kind of old thing is a poor person's gadget, not a snob's accessory. They don't know that the more important you are, the less you check your phone.. They don't know that rich Americans send their children to schools where there are no iPhones or Internet. It's in a school like that that Odessa has enrolled her kids, who have no Facebook account. The parents are on guard. Having one's head glued to a screen all day never helped anybody get to the top of the scholastic and social competition. A Yale University study shows that Westerners spend more and more time in front of their screens and less and less time eating food: the demise of a certain art de vivre.

With their shapeless jeans and their Quechua polar fleece jackets, François and Frédéric are not *fashionistas*. One is a tall mutant guru with long white hair in a ponytail, and the other is a compact little guy who looks remarkably like Lenin. Like the father of the revolution, his small eyes are tight. I really like Lenin's tight little eyes, a detail that's both frightening and exciting. I avoid looking at the guy with small eyes. I'm here to work, not to shudder.

We all address each other informally, as though we have known each other for a long time. Everything's simple, because the Guru has figured out what's left-wing and what's right-wing. I find out that the metro ticket is left-wing, as are family welfare benefits and the *jambon-beurre* baguette sandwich. He gets on my nerves, this guy, with his peremptory classifications. What about geraniums? And the raccoon? I point out that he's using a smartphone made by Apple, a monopolistic multinational company. And that the gesture that this piece of equipment requires, pinching the screen to take things, implies the idea of complete world domination. Typically, a right-wing object, no? There, a kick right back in the teeth. Speaking of which, are dentures right-wing or left-wing?

That doesn't make them laugh. Our trainers are serious. That's normal; they took part in May 68 and had intimate links with the idea of revolution. They had plenty of time to believe in it all the way, without worrying about such petty problems as looking for work. Afterwards, the ones who got back in line (meaning most, except François and Frédéric) dealt with money and social success with the same rational mentality. They left the next generations, meaning us, with the feeling of having been born too late, after the party was over. When we were born, the table had already been cleared. That lag explains our innate sense of irony, a form of humor that consists of being tongue-in-cheek in every situation. When you've always got a reason to laugh, you rarely have a reason to rebel.

We get to work. Everybody takes turns speaking. There's no exercise more destabilizing than to speak about yourself in front of others. I'm far from my comfort zone. I know how to chat about pretty much anything, because that's what the upper classes learn in school, but I don't know how to talk about myself in public. I decide to introduce myself and see what happens. I say: "Hello, my name is Corinne, I come from a privileged milieu" ... Our trainers look at me worriedly. I immediately backpedal, and quickly mumble: "Privileged because my parents weren't rich, though they read books". There's a palpable sense of relief in the audience.

The other trainees are more talented at left-wing public speaking. Especially Samia, who speaks without pathos about her hassles. She finishes her pitch with a song that she accompanies on the guitar, and it's beautiful. To think that I studied piano for years and that I'm incapable of playing a single tune...

It's my turn again. We have to express ourselves on the subject of: tell me who you are and who's oppressing you. (Note that nobody ever says I oppress, you oppress, we oppress.) I jump in. I describe how I joined the ranks of the self-employed, of those who are paid by the task. I make 2 euros on a book that's sold between 15 and 20 euros. I'm joining forces with the 700-euro generation, with the temps who get used like Kleenex, with those who are excluded from the wage-earning workforce, with the losers of history. As the self-proclaimed drama queen of the Uberized, I give it my all.

Given that I have a semi-consenting and semi-hostage audience, I take advantage of it. How nice it is to moan, to complain. I never had the right to complain, my parents didn't allow it. I can still hear them yelling: "Enough moaning!" as soon as one of us dared to feel sorry for ourselves. I deserve a standing ovation. Someone has fallen asleep: the audience is ungenerous, that's all.

The second step consists of describing class relations and mobilizations from a Marxist standpoint. It's a much easier exercise for me. The writer is a subcontractor, and as such, he's sub-contracted: most of the money goes into other people's pockets. It's enough to rise up and unfurl the red flag. Speaking of red flags, some people brandished it in May 1968. It was a time when you didn't pull any punches or keep quiet. Michel Butor, Nathalie Sarraute, Jean-Pierre Faye and others occupied the Authors' Society. It is a bureaucratic institution whose purpose escapes me, and probably escaped them too, because nothing came of it. Unfortunately for him or her, the author, that incorrigible individualist, is a bad revolutionary. Incapable of getting organized and mobilized, he deserves to stay destitute.

Finally, we need to analyze a current-affairs subject from a dialectical standpoint. Mine is obviously the centennial of the Russian revolution. It interests nobody in the book world. Censorship? Not even. Worse, much worse: indifference! That magnificent month of October 1917, which pulled history by the hair, is good for the scrap heap. It's the fault of the capitalists, they got a stranglehold on the world but it's not enough, they have to eat up the revolution, too. Management revolution, data revolution, it's the only word they ever use. The businessman Xavier Niel says he expects just one thing: revolution... There's another one. But it's not the same as my revolution. Sorry, ours. Phew, it's over. I'm exhausted. Being left-wing is no picnic let me tell you.

Right after a left-wing meal of *fougasse* flatbread and cardoon gratin, I join Samia in the room that we share. I think I'll make her feel good when I say:

"Samia, you should be on *The Voice!*"

She would be popular on *The Voice*, in every sense of the word.

To my great surprise, she shrugs:

"It's for dumb girls."

Snobbery is not just a characteristic of the rich.

We chat. I talk to her about Marco; she talks about her Ryan. And both of us reinvent the world. Who said there was no more social mixing? I feel closer and closer to the people. Samia and I play out *La Grande Illusion*, the famous Jean Renoir movie about class struggle. It describes the friendship between men of different social extractions, who get to know each other as prisoners during World

War I. The original script had an extra scene: two of the protagonists arrange to meet after the war in a fancy Paris restaurant. On the given day, the two chairs remain empty, with no indication as to whether the men gave up socializing or whether they were killed. A great popular movie, even if it leaves you hungry for more.

In real life, there's no question of staying thirsty.

"Samia, what if we drank something?"

"I checked, there's nothing."

"What do we do?"

"We get out of here, chick?"

"Let's go. There's got to be a minibar somewhere!"

We visit the rooms, nothing. Desolate. There's not even a minibar to raid.

"Hey, this place sucks," she proclaims.

"Look outside," I tell her, "the sky is full of stars."

Is the sky left-wing or right-wing? Is it just... popular? The air is cold and transparent. With the help of the joint she hands me, I understand the origin of the word "milky way." The smoke plants mines in my brain, and brings the following truth to my lips: a giant sprinkled droplets of milky and shiny sperm throughout the universe, and that's why the universe is littered with stars. It all makes sense now.

"I find that gross," she says.

Samia is looking down. It's time to use a word she taught me:

"You're right, we don't give a rat's ass about the sky." Lady Fortune gave me a talent for foreign languages.

Our alcohol raid has failed. Might as well go to bed.

"Come, let's kip."

Before falling asleep, Samia gives me a piece of common sense advice: "Forget the guy you're with right now, he's a wimp."

She's got a point. This story, left-wing or not, is off to a bad start. How do I know? Instinct. An animal instinct that comes from the depths of this gut, which I take such good care of.

When I get back to Paris, the days go by. I have no appetite left, and not a penny to my name. Here I am in the red, in more ways than one. To have to beg for sustenance: a disaster. Too bad, life isn't just about the Russian revolution. In a moment of discouragement, I move the "Red" file to the "Miscellaneous" category, that writer's junkyard. If I want food on the table, I have to find a commercial idea, something that sells. Let's be pragmatic. Nobody ever got rich writing about the revolution, Russian or not.

Montreuil, April 30th, 2016: the dessert

And on the love front, what to do? Should I get back in touch with Marco? No, it's up to him to get in touch. Or not? After all, he's the one who ran away to Turin. Even though he withdrew his artillery when I attacked. What if ... he was afraid of me? In the end, that would be funny. A bomber who weasels out... To think that I don't even know if our skin is compatible (sex organs have a life of their own, like mouth organs). There's nothing worse than those novels where the protagonists only make love in the last chapter, after hundreds of pages of foreplay as an appetizer.

Finally, I get an email from him. Proof that there is a God for the Reds. "I'm in Paris, I know you're often in town...I'm invited to a debate on the Italian left at the *Chaudronnerie*, in Montreuil. See you tonight, dearest."

It's not a surprise; I had tracked him down on the Internet. I would have liked him to warn me in advance. He who masters time masters circumstance, so he's ahead of me. I hesitate. Not to go, as a demonstration of independence? I'm not one to come running at the slightest snap of the finger.

I'll go, of course. How will I dress? At first, I choose the "no-frills tall girl" look, a pair of jeans and sneakers with a trendy T-shirt, the kind that goes with everything. A restrained style, because elegance means exercising visual imperialism. At the last minute, I change my mind. I split the difference: I keep on the jeans and go for a sexy top. What color? I rummage through my suitcase. I hesitate. Yellow? It's the color of traitors, of strikebreakers. Pink? Too girly. Orange is out of the question, I am not a Ryanair hostess. As for bright red, absolutely not: only little boys and old men wear it.

I go for blue, a right-wing color, but it's a dark blue, more rebellious than navy blue. It's an allusion to Monica Lewinsky's famous dress, sprayed with a squirt of presidential sperm. I put it on. No lipstick: it gives you a bitch's mouth. No sweater draped over the shoulders: it's too preppy. Feeling cold is better than committing a fashion faux pas. I put on my high-heeled ankle boots and look at myself in the mirror: I'm very thin, so everything's fine. I'm careful; my slimness is a precious social asset. Obesity is a shameful sickness among the rich. As long as my legs look like string beans inside my ultra-tight slim jeans, everything will be alright. I'm the queen of the night.

The debate takes place in an abandoned workshop at the heart of what was once the red belt, that cluster of Communist towns that had surrounded Paris since the 1920s. To get there, I rent a folding bike. Bike rental stores have sprung up everywhere, even in Paris's Golden Triangle. If the bourgeois prefer to rent rather than buy, it's a sign that we've moved into a new era: to own? What for? Ownership means a lot of worries: my family knows all about it.

The weather is stormy. Paris's breath is heavy with a faint licorice taste. I cross town from west to east, and cross the ring road. The metamorphosis of the red belt into Northern Lights aimed at illuminating the world has paved the way for dead factories, hasty warehouses, and dusty streets full of repulsive buildings. And new buildings for those who gave up dreaming of revolution a long time ago, and who only dream of social climbing, of luxury buildings with terraces and parking, of four-by-fours and private swimming pools. The middle class, the class that only knows itself and believes it has no limits, has popularized the aberrant idea that "there are no social classes." This absence of political awareness is appalling. I jot down on my to-do list: launch into an impassioned diatribe on the subject.

I arrive unfashionably early at the *Chaudronnerie*. If punctuality is the politeness of kings, it's also the servitude of rebels, because what would have happened if on October 24, 1917, at 9 p.m., the sailors of the Aurora cruise ship hadn't fired the most famous shot in history, the one that triggered the assault on the Winter Palace?

Nothing, just nothing, sadly nothing. No revolution. We would have drawn a blank.

The entrance ticket is a voluntary contribution. You give whatever you want to cover the costs. I imagine that the abominable bag-in-box wine container that sits on a table didn't cost very much. I give 10 euros, it may seem a detail to you, but to me it means a lot. It represents a meal at the *Café des Amis*, the bistro in the 16th where I eat when my roommate is not around. (I refuse to invite someone who refuses to invite me.)

It's an old-fashioned bistro, with a zinc counter, tiles on the floor and brown imitation leather seats. A haven of resistance to the wave of trendiness that is progressively nibbling up Paris. As in Toronto or in Barcelona, armchairs and sofas are slowly disappearing from restaurants, replaced by uncomfortable seats that accelerate customer rotation.

At the *Café des Amis*, there are only five shaky tables, and the menu is cheap. It serves a bourgeois and jovial cuisine, *Blanquette de veau, Coq au vin, Bœuf bourguignon, Paupiette...* Wholesome dishes that exude the dignity of a job well done. Their specialty is Chicken Marengo, its tender flesh stuffed with the cooking juice and draped in a brown sauce: that cornerstone of the dish. They excel at this dish, which was savored by Napoleon on the night of the eponymous battle, won with panache by the Austrians near a village in Italian Piedmont.

Tonight, the battlefield of love awaits me. I will prevail, just as Julien Sorel did when he set out to conquer Madame de Rênal and high society in *The Red and the Black*. Me, I go after the lower classes. I wonder what precautions we have to take when we visit the natives: Doctor Livingstone, I presume ? My success will depend on a mix of luck, talent and audacity. Fantasy is the privilege of players, the rest stick to being practical and prosaic. Emotion is at a peak, and it's spoiling my appetite. If this carries on, I'm going to die of starvation, the worst possible death. Come now, a risk-free life isn't worth living. I have nothing to lose; I jump right in.

It is time to rise to the fight ; I enter the big building. In the former tin-producing workshop, a couple dozen people have already arrived. The usual fauna composed of leftists, anti-globalization activists, neo-rurals, tattooed post-punks, members of a bakers' cooperative, dreadlocked hippies, young Christ-like rebels. A real leftorama. Some know each other and form whispering groups. There is more human heat here than in many *dîners en ville*. Who said there was no life on planet Marx?

I see Marco nowhere. I sit in the back. With its imposing structure, its metal beams and its ceiling height, the building has strong potential. It would be easy to turn it into an elegant contemporary home with moveable angles. It would be more interesting than the interior renovations of shameless parvenus, those who destroy centuries of patina and get glowing write-ups in home decoration magazines.

The audience around me is composed chiefly of the young and the old; the generation in between, to which I belong, is thinly represented. Not surprising: it's rare that people of my age should become politically engaged, militant. If they get into politics, most of them do it out of calculation, to get on the gravy train, to snatch jobs and cushy positions. Nobody's fooled; they're depoliticized to the core. Committed, uncommitted.

Never has history spawned a more listless generation. We grew up after disco, which taught us to fear big ideas. We would have liked to disobey, but we're too lazy to throw stones. We would have liked to raise our fists, but we're afraid to be ridiculous. We would have liked to climb on top of barricades, but only to take selfies. We would have liked to change the world, but where's the instruction manual? Are there any fact sheets? We're as carefree as patients who survived a scary and dangerous operation, that of our complete detachment from history. And that's how food replaced revolution, how the fork and knife defeated the hammer and sickle. The knife is no longer clenched between the teeth; it's placed to the right of the plate. Very much to the right.

Conversations circle around the labor law, which makes dismissals easier. For the past few weeks, this reform has caused an uproar among all of France's mutineers, fanatics, indignants, insurgents. If the cork hasn't yet popped, it's because it's a slow-combustion bomb with powerful earth-shaking potential.

Finally something happens, after so many years of morosity and disengagement. In the history of France, there were the revolutions of 1789, 1830, 1848, 1870, the semi-revolution of 1968... Then nothing. Dead calm. Dreary years of opportunism, of waiting games, of wheeling and dealing...Lenin, wake up; they've all gone soft.

Yesterday, I rushed over to the Place de la République. Finally an occupation of a square that's worthy of the name, comparable to that of the Puerta del Sol in Madrid, to Syntagma Place in Athens. Or of Wall Street, blocked by the angry Occupy Movement protagonists in 2011. Ah, Paris rising up, alight, excited...You could feel the insurrection coming. It won't take much to light the fuse that will inflame everything and bingo! The old world would be swept away in a swift and supple gesture. Like a golf swing.

Thousands of indignant people had converged on the big rectangular square. The air reeked of the sticky smell of kebabs, but also of something that took you by the throat, something more interesting, more dangerous. What could that possibly be? It reminded me of the smelling salts that corseted duchesses once used to stop themselves from fainting. In fact, it was tear gas. My first whiff of tear gas! A real baptism of fire, which should have been celebrated properly, and certainly not with a can of cheap beer. Yesterday, all I was missing was an ID check - what's the police doing?

Caught in the glue of a compact crowd, I elbowed my way over to the clunky monument sitting at the center of the square. The Republic is represented by an overweight lady who holds a branch in her hand (Provençal herbs for the kitchen?). It's a real tiered cake, this dessert shaped like a statue or a famous building. Antonin Carême is its inventor; Napoleon loved these themed pastries and ordered them for his banquets.

I would make an excellent history teacher. In my situation, I wouldn't scoff at a stable job and some job security, even if it's not a very glorious objective. It's good for those whose only aim in life is to enjoy the privileges of civil servants, to collect the peaceful pensions given to teachers. If I were a teacher, I'd live in a little house in the provinces and I'd have private medical insurance; I'd wear Capri pants and Velcro sandals and I'd vote socialist. The glamorous life.

At that point, I walked around the Statue of the Republic clockwise to make sure I was in the direction of history. And I ran very fast to leave the old world behind. "Down with the law! Down with work! Let's break everything! Even bread!" Let it be said, the revolution won't go hungry. With my Nike shoes, I could have gone faster, improved my performance, but it would have shattered the political coherence of my action.

The square teemed with tents, an orchestra, anti-pubs, a canteen, djembe players, punks with dogs, guerilla gardeners, an infirmary, Mexicans, a radio set, a fire breather... And also a loose cannon who yelled: "Let's share the blood and body of Capital" by raising his Coke can and wolfing down a hamburger.

Everybody is talking about the project of setting up a vegetable patch in the square; I remember having read that in Leningrad, during the first summer of the siege, the slightest green space was cultivated. The Up All Night movement gains new ground every day; everyone starts enjoying the participative debate. The Up-all-nighters get together in committees (Up All Summer, Up All Culture, Up All Over the Globe, Up in Exile, Up in the Media, Up in Popular Education). The talk is of the world that lies ahead, but there's no Writing committee. The writers stayed in bed. As I said, they have no sense of commitment and of collective action.

In Montreuil today, everybody is on edge. A plastic cup in hand (even empty, it gives me sustenance), I park myself next to a group and I bellow, "This law, how stupid." Protesting is good for you; it allows you to bring out your negative impulses. To tell you the truth, the labor law doesn't concern me. Family pressures and the weight of education are too strong; obeying a boss is social failure for an entrepreneur's daughter. How can Odessa look herself in the mirror when she gets her pay slip? Her salary must help sugar the pill. Between us, if more people in the workplace bit the hand that fed them, we might not need a revolution.

I jump in, and join the conversation.

"Hi, I'm Corinne (thanks, Dad, and this time I really mean it). I come from Belgium, where there's a law to make the job market more flexible. We're mobilizing against it."

Actually nothing happens, the Belgian rarely protests. Anyway, that's it; I'm speaking the language of my new comrades. I'm one of them. I have a foothold on the left bank of the world, without tripping, without collapsing on shore as I get off my yacht. Still, I have to be careful not to do too much; it would be a populist move (populist: use the word with caution, because it's become an insult. It initially referred to the tactics that flattered the people; it now refers to all those who shake up conventions in politics.)

"My name is Patrick. You're right; any excuse is good to limit the rights of wage earners. That's not the way it's going to work," says a guy with a pair of khaki pants, who carries socks in his braided leather sandals. My God, it is as to serve a Sauternes wine with a cassoulet, it doesn't match. But I like men who keep a stiff upper lip, who believe in something. A woman looks at me and chimes in:

"You see, in 2010, we went on strike for several weeks, then we won our case at the Labor Courts, with a fair amount of money at the end of it all. Now if the labor law is voted in, it won't be possible. By the way, I'm Barbara."

The call for sabotage that will spark everything off is an irresistible urge. I raise my voice:

"Why didn't you throw a spanner in the words, without leaving a trace? Cut the wrong cable? Make a task that takes only a few hours last for days?"

"Anarchists do this. It would have been used against the strikers," she replied calmly.

I went on:

"And what if you'd introduced a piece of malware in your company's server, without leaving a trace? Israelis know how to do that very well. Look at their Stuxnet computer virus and how it messed up the Iranians!" The eye of Moscow looks at me, appalled. Leftists hate Israel, that post-colonial country that exploits Palestinians and lives on American money. 'Boycott Israel' is their motto. It would be fun to see their faces if they knew that part of my family lives there - the part that doesn't live in New York.

Patrick rushes to my rescue.

"Corinne is right in principle. To be heard, you sometimes have to resort to sabotage," he reasons.

"But afterwards, there's a backlash, and police violence stinks," somebody says.

"We won't give up a thing," yells another. "Watch out for the uppercut, for the knock-out punch!"

Patrick has a little bit of a belly, but he has a cute, naughty little dimple when he smiles. What if this guy was a plan B ?

We sit on the benches provided by the local state school. MDG has still not arrived. The projection starts. The film is all about the extreme left in Italy and its various ramifications: Potere operaio (workers' rights), Lotta Continua (the struggle continues), Prima Linea (front line), the Red Brigades, etc. The viewer gets entangled in obscure political squabbles between the various factions. The problem with leftists is that they spend their time fighting each other. And the people who express themselves in the film would probably have been more convincing if they had adopted the TED talk format, these standardized speeches of "those who change the world"...

Suddenly Marco walks in and sits discreetly on the other side of the bench that I'm seated on. He doesn't see me, and sits next to Barbara. He leans over and whispers to her for a long while. There's a companionship there, it's very clear. Maybe even more than that... He takes her by the arm. And what if she were his friend, or his girlfriend? In any case, she can't be his wife, because no one has the right to proclaim himself the owner of another person by a marriage deed, that hidden ownership deed. Jealousy sends my heart into a spin, I don't want to be second best, the substitute, the frozen hake that you buy when you can't afford fresh fish.

I check out Barbara from the corner of my eye. Her short hair has a boyish part in the middle, and her hair is messy. She wears a T-shirt with no bra and she's flat as a board. She wears a high-waist, straight pair of jeans, a military jacket, and a scarf that's knotted like a keffieh. Her hands are not manicured, and if she's wearing makeup, you can't tell (nude make-up, as *Vanity Fair* would put it?) Maybe that's the left-wing swagger, being uglier than in real life – whereas the right-wing swagger is being more attractive than in real life.

Barbara may have contributed to defeating the employers' union, but she's no Latin bombshell. I have no intention of competing with someone so ugly that, on top of it is socially inferior: I have a habit of being a trophy. If this is how it's going to be, then Marco and I won't be the Great Red Couple. I live with it. The couple, that bourgeois invention, quickly turns into a deadly bore, almost as inedible as a French fry that's been reheated three times. This Great March across the land of sexual frustration, this place where the love we share is reduced to a miserly meal, that won't be us.

A little bit of amorous Realpolitik is necessary in my situation. Why not envisage a threesome? When there's enough for two, there's enough for three. Threesome love is the embodiment of the Socialist utopia of sex, with shared sexual responsibility and a redistribution of sexual positions. Lenin shows the way. He had a Spartan wife; Nadezhda Krupskaya (Krupskaya is pronounced by rolling the 'r,' to sound more Russian and make even more noise) never stopped Lenin from being in love with his elegant mistress Inessa Armand.

Outside the building, a few people smoke rolled cigarettes (Dunhills: right-wing; Riz-Lacroix: left-wing). I hear laughter: is there a leftwing sense of humor and a rightwing sense of humor? Hypoglycemia is the mother of melancholia and I head for the buffet. Buffet is a very big word. There are potato chips, pretzels, and nuts laid out on a Formica table. And even... some crackers. Awful. *Camarade gastronome*, help! The 16 little evil eyes on the crackers' pale faces stare back at me. I hadn't come across them in a long time. I didn't miss them. In the hierarchy of desirable food, the cracker is all the way at the bottom, just before the kitchen oilcloth. Mao was a thousand times right when he warned that the revolution was no gala dinner...

The debate drags on and is about the Mitterrand doctrine, that commitment made in 1985 not to extradite activist refugees in France. I see Marco walking off the podium. He eyes me intently, I feel it, I know it. I pretend to pour more wine. As I open the plastic faucet of the bag-in-box container, he lunges at me. I almost bang into him as I turn around. A maneuver worthy of a true strategist: lead him to believe that he's the one running after me.

He looks moved. If he finds me irresistible, I win.

"You're avoiding me, it looks like."

"Not at all. The place is cool, the decoration is first-rate, and the movie is sharp and piercing..."

I act like the resident pom-pom girl, I smile, I express myself. I know that everything is going to be played out now. To eat or to be eaten, that is the question. He looks at me, and I'm desperately tempted to lunge at him, to bite his lips with a hungry and reckless mouth.

He's at a loss for words. Is he going to spit it out?

"Corinne, I..."

He says something I don't hear, because the audience is getting up and chatting loudly: the talk is over.

I drag him into the only unreasonable place where we can hide, the bathrooms. You can't go wrong, there's only one stall. He throws me against the wall. His fingertips send a shower of sparks down my skin. His hand runs up my neck, I stop breathing. His tongue rolls over mine. This time, my breath is irreproachably fresh. One of his hands works its way over my chest, and his fingers rub my erect nipple through the fabric of my top. It's a post-fascist moment: defeat of the proletariat, offensive of the proletariat. Is this one going to dip his wicks in the cauldron of capital?

Highly unlikely because my partner is not the Nijinsky of striptease. He's getting tangled up in my bra strap. My breasts stay trapped in their lace barricade. But his hand goes ambushing into the elastic fabric of my pants and, back and forth, back and forth, makes me take off like an intercontinental ballistic missile R-7 Semiorka. Meanwhile, I massage his bottom, knead his crotch. We're in open country, he didn't bolt the door, and the moment has a sense of improvisation and freedom about it.

I would like to warn the comrade reader, whose modesty risks being upset by the scene that follows: it's not very true to the cannons of Soviet realism. He or she can therefore censor it, even if frank discussion of physical love seems to me a necessary precondition to a just and perfect society.

The rules of sexual etiquette within the red belt are unknown to me, but certain things are universal and transcend the right-left divide. The little treat offered by amateurs of aniseed lollipop can safely be classified as both right-wing AND left-wing. I stick my tongue in the scrub of his fly. The spread of oral sex since 1970 has contributed to democratizing fellatio. Driven by a spirit of sexual generosity, I don't practice it reluctantly. But I have a nagging hygiene-related thought at the back of my mind: Mao's personal physician, Dr. Li Zhisui, revealed that the Great Helmsman, who had a venereal disease, contaminated numerous women. Is there a risk of contracting *trichomonas vaginalis* through the mouth? (Hello, Professor T.?)

Tant pis, I like to live dangerously. I cover my teeth with my lips, as if to eat an ice cream from Berthillon, the famous ice cream place on the Ile de la Cité in Paris. I make an 'O' shape with my mouth, like the O of Soviet, of Communist. I salivate, I moisten, I give tongue lashes from the base. Then I take his penis into my mouth.

I make a slow circular movement, right-left, up-down, the right way. At that precise moment, I remember the words of Stalin who, to gauge the enemy's strength, would ask: "How many divisions?" I ask myself: "How many centimeters?" My voracious mouth turns into a measuring cup, that kitchen utensil that's used for ingredients. As far as my tongue can tell, it's a Herta Knacki sausage, at most. Never mind, this scepter will not be my personal trophy. When you're left-wing, you give up on the desire to own.

His Kalashnikov is already going fizzzzzz. The revolutionary smoothie has a disappointing taste, similar to that of Philadelphia cheese spread. While there's not enough there to heat up the taste buds of pleasure, 100 million left-wing sperms per milliliter are not to be turned down. This invigorating stream rids me of all material carnality, of any vain desire to conquer. That's it; I've had my leftist baptism.

We come out of the stall by putting on an air of detachment. I hope I don't have any traces on my chin; it would be an international shame. Oops, I have a stain on my clothes. I run back into the bathroom. With an imperious strike of the hip, I push a brown beauty who's putting on more makeup far away from the sink. She should get out; freshening up is not a militant act. I look scary; I'm pale as a smear of yoghurt drying in the sun. Bad food, pale skin. I rub away by splashing water all over myself...but the nectar gets embedded.

Just as I'm leaving the *Chaudronnerie*, Marco stops me:

"You're leaving?"

"Yes."

I unfold my bike. With his Brezhnevian eyebrows, he frowns.

If the Communists disapprove this means of transportation, the environmentalists have endorsed it. I'm starting to make out the specific differences in point of view that are as many dividing lines in the red (Communist) - green (environmentalist) - black (anarchist) galaxy. Being left-wing is more complicated than being being right-wing, so it's much more interesting. I look forward to fascinating debates with my new comrades. Now, I have the intellectual references to prevail in the verbal jousts that leftists so enjoy. If necessary, I'll go all the way to clash point, as nothing beats arguing with friends.

The sky is yellowish and lumpy, and is threatening to liquefy. Before I hop on my bike, I check that I've kept Patrick's phone number in my handbag.

MDG asks coolly:

"Are you coming back to Turin one of these days?"

"We'll see."

As the African saying goes, a swallowed cake does not have taste anymore. I give Marco a gentle kiss on the cheek. He doesn't expect it, and practically jumps. As I give my first push on the pedal, he mutters:

"I like it when it's impossible."

Exactly like Stendhal, who loves impossible love stories, because what's possible always ends up collapsing like a soufflé. In the end, Marco is maybe more Stendhalian than Marxist.

I retort: "I like having my mouth full."

All things considered, I'm more Marxist than Stendhalian: what counts is the materiality of things, the state of productive and especially reproductive forces.

I got the last word, that's already something. You should be wary of the bourgeois, they always end up taking something from you.

Desperate for a change of scene, I pedal as fast as I can. At that very moment, my cellphone rings. It's Patrick.

"What, you're gone already? I wanted to give you a ride in my car."

Not only is he left-wing but he's also nice. I guess he's a good egg who, when spending the night with a girl, serves her breakfast in bed the next morning. He's probably too thoughtful for my taste. Not the type you can live the *appassionata* with, that fire that tears the ground open, ravages the heart, unscrews the head and stirs the bowels.

"No thank you. See you next week? I'm going to a fancy dinner on Thursday. I warn you: people who are loaded are boring. But we may eat well. Come as you are."

Paris, May 5th, 2016: the petits fours

At the end of the street, I catch sight of the Robespierre metro station. This is where I asked Patrick to pick me up. I think cautiously of Robespierre the Incorruptible, champion of the French Revolution, who dared proclaim: "Champagne is the poison of liberty."

I fold my bike and Patrick helps me put it in the trunk, already crammed with tools and various bits of equipment. It looks like he raided the Castorama DIY store. Patrick belongs to the socio-type of the DIY enthusiast; he would look perfect with a cap pulled tightly over his head and a jigsaw in his hand. He has the intelligence of the hand, which is after all as good as any other kind of intelligence. With a toolbox, he'd look very much like the type who'd say, "I'm here to unplug your drain." A useful manual skill set which, if properly valued, would spare me the repulsive reading of how-to manuals.

I quickly dismiss these bad thoughts worthy of an exploitative capitalist and replace them with a Soviet vision. I picture myself a sickle in hand - in the middle of a crowd that chants and cries in a single voice - moving with acrobatic impetuosity. As I reap a field, Mr. Drain comes over to give me a chaste kiss; a hammer pokes out of his overalls. I wear an adorable cotton apron with a floral white-and-blue pattern and a red border.

His car is a yoghurt tub with a license plate from the outer suburbs. I have no idea what kind of car it is; I'm incapable of distinguishing these machines. In any event, they're all the same color: grey. I never drove, which spares me the ultimate in boorishness, getting angry at the wheel. Cars are so passé. His is a trash can. I have a hard time fitting my legs between a sack of cement and empty pizza cartons. A green deodorant pine tree hangs pointlessly from the rear-view mirror.

"What do you do?" asks Mr. Drain.

"I'm a writer. It's a profession where you're paid by the job. The profession is not organized; we get ripped off. It's a bit like milk producers who sell at a loss while the big retailers and the food industry manufacturers get fat."

My full-immersion training came in handy.

Then Patrick speaks to me about himself. He's a social worker and he's on training leave to become a "social engineer." I have no idea what that means. Does that sector award a real diploma? I'm certain of one thing, it's not a job opportunity for the nation's elites. Fortunately, I recently learned that diplomas are an invention of the dominant used to exclude the dominated. I have to be careful not to let class contempt seep in between Mr. Drain and myself).

His conversation is a mix of weather babble, little jokes, and self-deprecation. Is this flirtation? An ambiguity in line with the seduction code that prevails everywhere both to the left and to the right. I keep quiet. I meditate seriously by looking at Paris, the city that was the cradle of every revolution, yet always failed to bring one to fruition.

We pass through Place du Colonel-Fabien, site of the towering Communist Party headquarters built by Oscar Niemeyer. The S-shaped building snakes through this traditionally left-wing area. The Communist architect wanted to break with the verticality of the Paris of Haussmann, the architect who "modernized" by running the poor out of town. Communists are fashionable ever since no one votes for them anymore, and this futurist construction has become the inescapable scene of fashion weeks, of photo and advertising shoots.

The rain adds softness to the streets and a certain sheen to the colors of the night. We're getting close to the chic arrondissements of Paris, a centrifugal city where the richer you are, the more centrally you live. I quickly forget the refugees, the people we refer to as migrants, who are crammed under the elevated subway. It never hurt anybody to change countries. I'm a migrant myself, a borderless person who goes from Stendhal to Lenin. On my right, I notice the discreet, almost anonymous shop front of a starred restaurant that's on a roll and on the cover of the magazines. It's the place everyone is talking about: my gustatory fantasies center on this place. The cook revolutionizes the French culinary landscape. How I'd like to eat there!

My driver is not the ideal partner for this ruinous folly. By the way, what am I doing here, on the passenger seat of a car that's good for the scrap heap? I'm obviously cast against type, in a role where my social capital is not very handy. But this urban ride has the smell of novelty. It's a very long time since I rode in a car. What a transgression! Because driving at high speed contributes to polluting the atmosphere through the emission of tiny particles, those solid suspended compounds emitted by combustion, 10 times smaller than the thickness of one-tenth of a noodle, explained to me the bike renter, an ecologist wearing an "Extinction Rebellion" T-shirt. And whose fault is that, eh? Capitalism's, of course.

"It's a private dinner," Edouard told me on the phone. "Going to a restaurant is lame, the cool thing now is when the restaurant sets up in your kitchen." He gave me the address before adding, with a throaty little laugh: "You can come with a guest."

The street's rows of proud and imperturbable facades clearly indicate that it will take decades before the recession is felt there. Patrick and I enter a building that overlooks the Eiffel Tower. A maid immediately opens the door, the kind you don't see anywhere, clad in a black uniform, a headdress and an apron. She takes my foldable bike without saying a word and disappears. I look in the entrance mirror: I look older, that's confirmed.

Militancy has left its mark on my face. I feel like the dessert that was fashionable five years ago, the *cannelé* that was all the rage on the buffet tables, and that everybody has now tired of. Even if I'm improving, as a fine wine does, I'll soon be 40. Being in a bad mood is sexy for a youngster; it's heavy 20 years later. According to a Yale study, at 40, you're likelier to have a bomb fall on you than a man. What, midlife crisis, already? Facelift, no facelift? (Facelift = right-wing). I stick my tongue out at the mirror.

Mr. Drain looks around, feeling out of place in this ultra-bourgeois decor. The hostess appears. Fiftysomething, very upright in her dark-red jacket, she wears black trousers and a cream-colored blouse with a collar that's adorned with a very fine embroidery ribbon.

Haughty, the stuck-up lady of the house looks us up and down without a word, motionless. She seems to have been eaten away by her own sourness. Her carefully studied blow-dry gives off this sub-text: *I'm a blow dry but I refuse to be a blow dry that looks like a blow dry. My role is to enhance the natural, not to transform the hair into a handful of spaghetti stuck together.*

We have the impression of coming out of nowhere. We're both out of tune with the party, and we're breaking the codes: I'm wet as a dog that's been caught in the rain, my clean-and-not-even-torn jeans are not trendy and my bodysuit is stained (I have put on my clothes from the other day, my aunt's flat doesn't have a washing machine and there is no way I'm washing my clothes by hand). Patrick has a neglected look, with his disheveled bun, his lousy T-shirt and his grey hooded sweater.

"What's the plan, here?" mutters Mr. Drain.

"We're gatecrashing a rich people's party."

He looks puzzled. Even though I'd explained the concept of a high-society dinner to him. No, it's not like a soccer party with buddies. It is a very French tradition, very codified, combining pleasure with social spectacle. It is also a place for effective networking, which allowed Emmanuel Macron to become President of the Republic.

A pre-teenager with a studiedly laid-back look barges into the entrance hall. He walks right past without looking at me. He's wearing a fur shirtfront, a horn hat, and a red-and-black axe on his back. He's clearly planning to go to a Cosplay party.

Patrick exclaims:

"Skyrim!"

(Video games: left-wing or right-wing? I can't say. The Guru would have had the answer.)

The young man is surprised:

"You know the game?"

"Big time!"

"Hi, I'm Jean-Eudes. Can you help me please? I bought Dawnguard, I wanted to do the quests, and I ended up as a vampire lord. To get around in vampire lord mode is horrible. It's an unplayable class, a disgusting skinhead."

"I'm Patrick. I have a solution. You need to go to the Morthal tavern; you'll be directed to Falion who can take care of you. Where's your computer?"

He knows the password to break through the young man's glass bubble. The two geeks belong to the same tribe, and they disappear down the corridor, ignoring the hostess, who is still as motionless as a pillar of salt.

Some name-dropping should loosen the atmosphere. "We're guests of Edouard," I tell her. She then decides to accompany me to a large living room with white carpets, minimalistic furniture, monumental paintings and skillfully lit walls. The kind of simplicity that costs an arm and a leg. The décor serves as a backdrop to a decidedly non-conformist detail: between two silver candlesticks adorned with precious stones, a transparent plastic dwarf on a low side table that's giving the finger to the guests.

The hostess, Sybille - Bibi for short - introduces me to the company. She hesitates between "Mademoiselle Zed, Marcel's daughter (right-wing) and "Corinne, writer" (left-wing) and finally whispers "a friend of Edouard's." Everyone knows Edouard, to the point where his family name has become redundant: that's how popular he is. I mumble a quick hello, the bare minimum. I have no desire to either apologize for being late or speak to anyone. Even less to give a kiss. Then again, it would be fun, because it would be out of place among the dozen people present, mainly men who look fairly awkward, probably because they're hungry. We sure could use Lenin in this place, that ice-breaking vessel strong enough to slice through a sheet of ice three meters thick.

They belong to the same world. A European Commissioner, a banker, an entrepreneur, a media baron, a lawyer... (Hey, Professor T is not here?). "Instinctively I have always despised the bourgeois," wrote Stendhal. They look like the grey expanse of the Atlantic Ocean with the statue of Liberty on one end and the Bank of England on the other. The kind who feed on the *Financial Times* (I'm sure they linger over the "Lunch with" section, where a journalist interviews a VIP over a casual meal.) With a flawlessly natural air, avoiding any sartorial statements, they fade into the middle-class void. The middle-class is the center of everything, it is neither at the top nor below, neither to the right nor to the left, neither rich nor poor. Nevertheless, their boilerplate look is made up of a subtle mix of classic fabrics and a twist of neglected and bold micro-details. Those secret signs that go unnoticed to outsiders are intended for their equals. In the eyes of others, it's essential to go unnoticed. Being rich: is that the last taboo?

In a classic high-society dinner, you need a little variety, and tonight I'm the odd one here (I don't count Patrick, he's disappeared.) I feel as lonely as a slice of lemon in a diet Coke. The curtainless windows look out on the Parisian sky, cloudy and spotted with lightning. I go off to wash my hands. You recognize the genuinely wealthy from the splendor of their bathrooms: double washbasins carved from a single block of Italian granite, subtle lights that make you look good when you peer in the mirror, and a pebbled floor that's so clean you could eat on it. The thing with rich people's WC's is that you see yourself living in them.

When are we going to eat? The guests eye the avant-garde delights that have been skillfully prepared by the highly coveted Danish chef. He's the crème de la crème, a limitless creator of gourmet adventures. As the adrenalin reaches a peak, I join Edouard in a corner of the living room. He's really handsome, with his metallic blue eyes, his sensual lips and his straight nose. He looks good in his obviously classic, nicely cut, slightly wrinkled jacket. And he's wearing an incredibly wild tie where tiny deer are playing. Where did he find such an improbable accessory - at the flea market or in a really expensive upper-class store? It's both elegant and cheeky, an in-between space for irony, our shared language (his and mine).

"Hi Doudou."

"Hi Coco. You have a stain here..." And he puts his finger on my top.

We chuckle. Not too loudly though. Without seeming to, Edouard is here to do some work and engage in some networking. "The youngest french gallerist in New York" is all the rage in high society, and he's invited everywhere. Well, everywhere among the rich.

Pointing to Bibi, I ask him quietly:

"Edouard, who's this broad?"

"It's a favor being returned," he says carelessly. "She owes me a favor. She's an exhibition curator."

"Is that a real job?"

Curator means exhibition organizer. Curators are self-employed, glorified project managers, often getting paid peanuts. Bibi doesn't need money; art is a hobby for her, but a self-serving hobby because she has ambitions. She's aspiring to a position in the cultural industry and, as Antonin Carême wrote, "The good cooks, the saucepans and my skillful meal planners are more useful to the vision and the political mission than the secretaries or the written questions."

"I'll get you a drink," says Edouard, without answering my question, which isn't really a question.

I hear Bibi telling her guests:

"Furniture has a soul. I'm in tune with the sensibility of the objects around me, their affinity. I don't choose anything; they impose themselves upon me. I've made them mine; I've tamed them." I know what comes next: she will claim to have done it all on her own - before dropping the name of a high-profile decorator.

It's clear: the evening will be *pre-fascist*, as in, hoity-toity.

A waiter goes up and down the room carrying a platter of canapés. They're from Lenôtre; I noticed the empty boxes as I walked past the kitchen. (The service is not professional; the guests shouldn't know the supplier's name.) The quality has gone way down ever since Sodexho, an institutional catering multinational, the Titanic of taste, bought up the fancy caterer. Lenôtre is not what it used to be. Yet the rules of emergency gastronomy require that I make the best of a bad situation and feed on whatever's available where I am. So I peck and freshen up my mouth with champagne, which I enjoy in little sips. Mmmm...when it passes over the tongue, then eases into the throat, time freezes into as many glittery micro-eternities.

Champagne is hotter, more exuberant than love, after all. Love... gives wings to some, while others hit the ground, and I'm one of them. I'm sad when I'm living through passion, like those who get sad after a few drinks. In some people, passionate love takes the shape of a manic-depressive psychosis, alternating between excitement and depression. I'm sure Professor T. wouldn't recommend it for me. It uses up too much energy, time and emotion. This foolish race just means that you get taken for a ride before being tossed into a deep frying pan. Love is a Potemkin village: those trompe-l'oeil settlements hastily put together by a Russian general to impress Catherine the Great. Stendhal - who admitted: "My main occupation, or rather my only occupation, has always been love" - must have suffered a lot.

Can men and women work together - or might they be like peanut butter and chocolate, never to peacefully coexist? Now, I long for calm; a summer lake hiding under the surface of deep, cold waters, like in Scandinavian crime fictions. But if I cross out love, what am I going to think of to spice up my life?

The Eiffel Tower sparkles with all its lights. It looks like a giant Marilyn Monroe, covered in jewels, with her legs open to the caress of the Seine river breeze. Reality is only interesting when it carries nuggets of madness, so I address a fervent inner prayer to her: "Take off! From below to above, from the pavement to the blue sky! Use your steel slippers to shoot for the star-studded sky! Send us little bomblets of light between the eyes! Tear up the night with its tangle of violet hairs! May your incandescence carve space-time! Prove to us that everything is possible! Revolution, and even...love. May that bitter fruit one day become ripe and sweet."

Unwittingly interrupting my little telekinetic session, Edouard hands me a drink.

"You stink. Have you been drinking?"

"Worse: I ate some crackers a few days ago."

"You're going to mess up your stomach. Poor man's food seriously affects your health."

Appetite comes with eating, and a *foie gras* toast melts on my tongue. It's a little too soft, to be honest. What if it was reconstructed liver? No, they wouldn't dare give their customers something that has the texture of cat food. To be absolutely sure, I try the other canapés. Like the many-limbed goddess Shiva, I quickly grab an asparagus hors d'oeuvre, a carpaccio of scallops and a miniature vol-au-vent.

"How's your book coming along?" he asks as he dips his lips in his glass.

"It's not coming along at all."

"Mental block?"

"Social block."

"Any hope?"

"No. It's stillborn."

"And your love story? Did you get rejected?"

"Um...Let's just say that things got out of hand."

I really want to tell him about the Montreuil episode. Edouard would probably die laughing. Probably...but not necessarily.

"You're confusing a lightning war with seduction, I told you so. Who won the battle?"

"Um... Actually, it's game over."

"You know what Confucius used to say? Sex and food are two basic instincts. You should focus on the second."

It's hard for me to admit, but he's right; when you lose, you have to get up and leave the table.

"Thanks for the support. Omniscience must be a real burden for you."

I swirl the champagne twice in my glass before drinking half of it in one gulp. I want to be sure it goes to my head in one go, like the smell of cake filling a kitchen. I must remember to jot down the name of the winegrower. What if I was just re-gentrifying?

"It's your turn. Do you want Marco's email?"

"No need, I already got in touch with him," says Edouard calmly.

I thought he would chicken out. I sense the fleeting, sweetish taste of jealousy on my tongue. Not without a little bewilderment: who am I jealous of, exactly?

I try to tone down the hint of worry in my voice:

"Oh really? You didn't waste much time."

"I'm organizing an exhibition on *Arte povera*, that artistic movement that challenges consumer society by using sand, rags, soil, wood and used clothes. A beggar's art, in other words."

What a pain in the neck when it comes down to it, he too could be a teacher. I barely listen to him. *Arte povera* doesn't thrill me any more than *Cucina povera*, with its chickpea pasta and its cabbage cooked with bread. The leading vegetable is the *cime di rapa* (turnip greens), half broccoli, half-turnip: it used to be fed to pigs, now it feeds the rich. Why be austere when you can afford to be lavish? The next step is eating nettle and acorn. In the end, you won't eat anything at all. There are already workshops to learn how to fast, and they're very trendy, despite -or because- the lousy value-for-money ratio.

"What does *Arte povera* have to do with Marco?"

"Some artists in this movement are close to the far left. I asked Marco to be the exhibition's curator."

I'm staggered. Hard to imagine the revolutionary creating a spatial narrative and coming up with an exhibition design.

"Did he accept?"

"Yes. I'm meeting him in Turin so we can talk it over."

"Hey, you've left me speechless. It's going to go viral in New York."

"You bet! It's going to rock!"

"You'll be more contemporary than your contemporaries: Even super-contemporary... What's the name of the show?"

"'Infinito.' The word *Infinito* will be projected on a partition where it can't be read. To decipher it, you'll have to go to the infinity point."

"It's very 'post-...'"

Infinity, that vortex that engulfs everything in the whirlwind of its insatiable void: *pre or post?* I need another glass of champagne, right away. Three glasses, that's still acceptable, it's social alcoholism. Four, on the other hand, is alcoholism, period. As my grandmother said, it is necessary to live within the limits of decorum.

"Shall we eat?" mutters the hostess in a hushed voice. We head to the dining room as Jean-Eudes and Patrick reluctantly get up from the computer. Jean-Eudes looks like he's given up on the Cosplay party, even if he's still wearing the Skyrim costume that makes him look like a tacky Minotaur. In a few years, he will wear a suit and tie and sit on an executive board. Patrick holds a Fanta can in his hand, which is no problem for Bibi. Since he's charmed her son, she casts him a protective glance. Maybe she thinks he's a Silicon Valley wonder boy. For men, to be underdressed at a dinner party, is a sign that they belong to the changing establishment; the T-Shirt exclaims "we will bury all of you."

"Hello. What are we having?" Patrick unceremoniously asks the maître d' as he sits down. He ignores etiquette; it's a good thing I brought him along.

"Hello, Sir. We propose a single dish prepared especially for you this evening by chef Eluf Redzobi. It's a fish head from the Feroe islands cooked on a Yakitori-style wooden skewer topped with a touch of sugar-coated cod liver, accompanied by fried lichen and served on a bed of moss."

Tonight we're not just eating fish, we're sharing cultrual capital. I definitely won't be gaining weight with this; it's no surprise that rich people are thinner than the poor.

"To begin with, we have a tasting of Finnish caviar, straight from the tin, to be savored plain with its mother-of-pearl color scheme," continues the maître d'.

Patrick and Jean-Eudes look at each other. Patrick calls out to him:

"Big guy, are you up for it?"

"Hell, no," replies the young grouch, who's not at all big.

Patrick gets up and graciously declares:

"Monsieur, I'm sorry, but that's not gonna work for me."

He turns to Jean-Eudes, who also gets up from his chair:

"Shall we buy some fries and go after the dragons?"

The two gourmet hooligans disappear in a burst of laughter.

Someone sighs:

"Caviar is pigs' jam."

Edouard leans over me and points to Mr. Drain by raising his chin:

"That guy's really awesome. Who is it?"

"A leftist. I brought him here."

"What does he do, your leftist?"

"He's a social engineer. Don't ask me what that is."

"Social engineer... is that a real job?

The person sitting next to me, an entrepreneur in a tweed skirt and a Hermès scarf, addresses the guests, lowering her voice:

"I must sound ignorant, but what is the difference between

Finnish caviar and Russian caviar?"

The banker, an expert in the "Dutch sandwich", the tax optimization technique that enables big corporations to save billions of euros, butts in:

"You poor thing, there's no more Russian caviar. Sturgeon fishing has been outlawed in the Caspian Sea. Unfortunately, we will no longer eat Beluga, the Rolls-Royce of caviar..."

"It's the Communists' fault," someone suggests.

That's not the case. Stop falsifying historical facts; it's my job to set the record straight. I just read an article on sturgeon eggs in Vanity Fair's *savoir-vivre* section; that consumerist booklet comes in handier on hostile terrain than the *Communist Manifesto*. Even though caviar - the ultimate fantasy food, symbol of boisterous wealth - remains associated with going out on the town, the Commies exploited it with restraint.

"No, it's the capitalists' fault. It's at the end of the Soviet Union that uncontrolled fishing wiped out the Caspian," I forcefully declare.

The European Commissioner, who's about as rock-and-roll as a career in the regional civil service, has his own views on the matter.

"It's all a question of governance. To speak of the depletion of resources misrepresents the problem."

"What's a pity is that caviar today has lost its authenticity," sighs the banker.

"Breeding farms are everywhere. Sturgeon is no longer a fish; it's the UN. Soon, it will be as democratized as smoked salmon. Everything's falling apart."

I'm getting bored at this oh-so-chic dinner party, as warm as a fridge. It's time to spice things up:

"I don't like eggs. Eating an egg is killing the seed of life. I give up my caviar. Who wants some?"

It wouldn't take much to put it up for auction.

Bibi, who was so far unmoved, shoots me a dirty look. I'm not Corinne anymore, but a distasteful thing placed in the middle of the dining room. I've blacked out the conversation with my little dinner terror routine. There's a hushed silence. The guests stare at their Alessi cutlery. Edouard stands by me, more out of friendship's sake than out of ideological solidarity. I expected nothing less of him.

"I too give up mine. I hear it's horribly fattening: 264 calories per 100 grams! Not to mention the cholesterol on top of that...my dietician will kill me."

Opposite me, a man dressed in black whose face looks familiar takes up the caviar challenge.

"Caviar is a really divisive topic. We published an illustrated book on the subject, and it sparked a debate."

That's it, I recognize him, he's the very influential director of *Les Papiers*, a publishing house that he inherited and transformed into a multicultural and cross-media hub. This energetic man is active in a host of committees and bodies. His interpersonal skills will soon enable him to play a major role in the industry's restructuring around a few multinationals, according to the evening newspaper that wrote about him.

"Oh yes, I glanced at « *Beluga, our final frontier* ». They're amazing, these black beads photographed like planets."

"A real bestseller: we had to reprint it several times," he says.

"They always say that books don't sell," intervenes the banker. "They say publishing is doing badly, but some publishers have high margins, when they are owned by a multinational conglomerate with interests in trade book publishing, cable television, radio broadcasting, media distribution, political consulting, advertising, magazines..."

The Papiers director frowns indignantly:

"You've got the wrong idea. We're not soup vendors, the book trade is an occupation in its own right. It's really hard right now."

The book industry is an apostolate. To say that publishers get rich by selling books is a crime of lese-majeste. 'We believe in,' a much-repeated phrase in publishers' carpeted corridors, is a two-part message: 1) We don't do this for money; 2) We're not sure we can pay you, but since you don't do this for money either, it doesn't matter, does it? You're not greedy by any chance, are you, Corinne? That would really be disappointing."

After that, the conversation turns to banal topics. First, the rise of populism: it's beyond belief, the people who vote in spite of common sense. The people vote badly, we need to change the people. And then, ah, the wonderful Louis Vuitton Foundation in Paris, that crystal palace, that cathedral of light that showcases such subversive, daring works. Chutzpah, that's what's missing in our day and age. Balls, in other words.

The publisher leans over to me:

"You're Corinne Zed, right? I saw you in a France 2 program. You know, we're talent aggregators, and we'd be delighted to welcome you into our catalog."

"As it happens, I've got something cooking."

"What's it about?"

"The Russian revolution."

"Why not? I'd like to develop new areas of knowledge. And this would be a way for *Les Papiers* to position itself on the non-fiction market and gain visibility," he says, thinking out loud. I can picture him very well talking about merchandising, reprinting in China and digital marketing at a business meeting.

As for non-fiction, meaning essays, it was long somewhat looked down upon by publishers. Until they realized that the sector was more resilient to reader erosion than novels.

"The Russian revolution will be 100 years old next year."

I could do the article more aggressively, but the fighting spirit has left me. How do teachers do it, repeating the same thing year after year?

"Perfect timing. I don't know what you have in mind, but what seems relevant to me is a serious book. Something factually sound. Not a glorification, it's not in the spirit of the times."

He's suspicious, it's clear. He's afraid I will give the revolution mouth-to-mouth resuscitation, and then anything could happen.

"I know how to keep a distance from my subject matter without compromising my principles, of course."

"You're a historian, I believe? Good, with a topic like that, Les Papiers is eligible for a subsidy..."

Cherry-picking state subsidies: that's rich people's form of begging. Putting together the application, ensuring the support of potential allies, persuading commissions is an art. "Culture" editors know how to go about it, and the Republic is gullible.

"I'm at your disposal to talk things over."

I've compiled some notes and documentation, like a hamster with its jowls full of grain. I could finish "Red" in a few months. I want to put that behind me and move on to something else. Rush? No, get straight to the point; Stendhal wrote *The Charterhouse of Parma* in just 52 days.

"Are you free for lunch, tomorrow or the next day?"

Of course I'm free. I never miss an opportunity to get invited; you never know what tomorrow will bring. And I'm available every day. That's the beauty of being poor. The wealthy who spend their life going from meeting to meeting between time zones don't know what they're missing. I have time to sleep in, wander around the streets comparing bistro lunch menus. If you envy me, comrade reader, all you have to do is imitate me; anyone can be lazy. It's a matter of will, it's like everything else. But it's important to show that we're very busy. No one takes seriously those who have time, that is why so many people go through life with a smartphone glued to their hand.

-I'm very busy these days. I'll take a look at my diary to see if I can clear a spot at noon and I'll tell you very soon...

The main course is served. I thought I'd throw myself on the meal like I would on golden apples from the gardens of Hesperides. I was expecting fireworks, an explosive menu. It's puzzling, beyond gourmet, and ultimately, artificial. In cooking, you need to hear the chef's own voice, a coherent voice, and here, I can't hear anything. The show is in the plate, and that's the problem; normally, it should stick to the rules. I have a feeling that my tongue is made of cardboard. What if I was *orally* frigid? Now then, that would be very, very bad. That would be the end of it all.

Maybe it's the people sitting next to me that are ruining my appetite. They are talking about mergers and acquisitions, How is it that so many people could be interested in the business world, with its abstruse vocabulary, its acronyms, its figures, and its tricks worthy of Balzac's most boring chapters? To talk business at a dinner party is an unforgivable faux pas. It's time to leave what Stendhal called "the table of a bad book." Out of defiance, I don't finish everything on my plate. "Think of the starving little Africans," my parents would have said, refusing to admit that there were more obese than malnourished people on earth. They denied the despicable obesity epidemic that is drowning mankind in lard.

Without waiting for the dessert (mashed potatoes with plums), I sneak out behind Edouard, expected at another dinner party. He whispered some excuse in Bibi's ear who seems to be satisfied. My neighbors must be relieved, even if they have not expressed their olfactory discomfort. At this very moment the banker, his taste buds led astray by the Puligny-Montrachet, hollers: "If I were American, I'd vote for Bernie Sanders." The bad boy attitude is definitely all the rage in the higher social spheres. How far will he go to be provocative? I wonder whether he'll have the nerve, the balls to engage in dialectics on the armed struggle. That would be a change from the gossip that usually makes the rounds at these dinner parties (so-and-so is gay, so-and-so is dishonest).

Down the hall, in the room where Patrick and Jean-Eudes make orgasmic sounds in front of a screen, the dragon is in trouble. I wouldn't want to be in its shoes. Around the machine lie empty containers of French fries and bottles of Coke - not even Diet Coke. I enter and I see on a table a plate of petits fours, it is half empty. No, Patrick has not defected to the enemy: the pocket of his baggy pants reveals an adorned candlestick that has nothing to do here... I'd like to steal the other one, but I would have to go back to the dining room: no thank you.

"I'm sick of this dinner party, it's zombieland. I'm leaving."

It's a foregone conclusion; Patrick is not leaving before he's finished the game. Staring at the screen, he replies:

"I'll stay on a bit, you don't mind, do you?"

"No problem."

"We'll keep in touch?"

From the dining room doorstep, Bibi asks Patrick with a sweet voice:

"Patrick, you're at home here. And if you wouldn't mind checking out my PC (Personal Computer, not *Parti Communiste*), it would be lovely. Something's really wrong. Yes, yes, later, of course, later, we have all the time in the world. By the way, there's a guest room for the joystick warriors to get some rest..."

It's not that late. I remember just in time that Cherry is giving a little party to celebrate his departure for the complicated Orient. There are better ways to savor the taste of Parisian nights, but beggars can't be choosers. And plus, my cousin has lent me money; I might as well be nice and show some gratitude.

On the sidewalk, glinting with rain, the city appears in two colors, black and grey. My feet are hurting. This is the last time I'm wearing high heels, a form of torture worthy of feudal China, when women's feet were bandaged.

"Patrick's been requisitioned for a granny-sitting evening. He'll regret having come with me."

Edouard has another interpretation of events:

"You know, something could go on between the two of them... Old pots make the best soups," he adds with a chuckle.

"Bibi and Patrick, you think?"

I'm flabbergasted. I was choosy, and now it's too late. Life's not kind enough to offer you another helping.

"Do you want to bet?" asks Edouard.

Enough of silly bets. I bend over to unfold my bike.

"Good-bye, dear Coco. Are you going back to Brussels soon? "

"I've booked a blablacar next week."

"Maybe we'll meet again before, then."

"Good luck in Turin."

He smiles:

"We're entering the Age of Aquarius, it's the return of love."

No hard feelings. I blow him a kiss with the tip of my fingers.

I get on my bike, give a reluctant pedal stroke and, as the bicycle sways from left to right, I head to the Seine. I cross the Alexander III bridge, named after one of the last Russian Tsars, just as a big storm breaks out. I wonder what kind of advance *Les Papiers* will offer me. How much does the revolution cost? Probably not much, but given that I'm drunk, nothing matters. If I need money, I'll borrow some from Doudou. And then, the Eiffel Tower will take off really soon. And we will all climb on board, the poor, the rich, the new poor and the old money. And while I'm at it, even the new rich: alcohol makes you want to share.

I let myself be swallowed up by a grumbling raincloud. I can't wait to get safe and eat something. Finally I am still a little hungry.

Acknowledgements

This is a novel that takes place in existing places, from the Lenin Café to the Chaudronnerie via the Lingotto. The reader can enroll at the Marxist University, and go to the American Communist Party headquarters, but the Stendhal Encounters are pure fantasy. The mentioned works of art also exist.

My thanks to Marie-Paule for her encouragements and the connection with the Lenin Café; Cyrille for his help in writing the dialogues; Yves for going over the text with a fine toothcomb; the irreplaceable Manu for having imagined Edouard's wardrobe. I would also like to thank Carole and Philippe, who took the time to improve the text. And of course to Nazanine and Farah, elegant, multilingual globetrotters thanks to whom this book is now sailing off into the horizon.